MW00325827

For the Love

of Money

By:

Shoney K

Hustle2Hard Publications
For the Love of Money © 2012 by Shontell Kennard
All rights reserved. No part of this book may be reproduced in any form or by any means without prior consent of the Publisher, except brief quotes used in reviews.
ISBN-13 978-0-9860084-0-5
ISBN-10 0986008400
First Printing May 2012
Printed in the United States of America
10 9 8 7 6 5 4 3 2 1
This is a work of fiction. Any references or similarities to actual events, real people, living or dead, or to real locales are intended to give the novel a sense of realism. Any similarity in other names, characters, places, and incidents is entirely coincidental.

Dedicated to my daughter Destiny Davis and
Author Nate Nati Holmes R.I.P.
Babe, God has gained an angel. You're gone,
but never will be forgotten.
Hustle Hard...Real Rap...100!!!

Acknowledgements

First and foremost, it's only right that I thank GOD for blessing me with the gift to express myself through a pen. Despite the obstacles that I had to overcome, I continued to push. Without God on my side, I don't know where I would be. Giving all praises to the man upstairs.

To my daughter Destiny, you know Mommy loves you right? You're my first love. Everything that I do, I do it for you. I just want to say never give up on your dreams because anything is possible. You've been in my life 14 years and each year you make me a stronger person. Never be a follower, always a leader…Love you more than life itself.

To my beautiful mother Debra Kennard-Chandler thanks for having my back at all time. You have been through a lot within the last year. Continue to be the strong black woman that you are. Pops wouldn't want it any other way. R.I.P. John "My Pops" Chandler.

To my father Derrick Williams…just wanted to say thanks for creating a wonderful daughter…I love me some me….LOL and I love you, too.

To my one and only blood sister, Tiffany Kennard. I remember when you used to get on my nerves LOL, but I still continued to love you. You have turned into a beautiful young lady. Keep up the good work because you know Destiny is watching. Just like I've set positive examples for you, you have to set them for her. We are Kennard's and there is only one way for us to go and that's to the top. I love you dearly and thanks for blessing me with a beautiful niece Mia Myles.....Aunt love the baby.

To my #1 fan Timothy "Black" Rayford. For the last five years, you have been very supportive no matter what journey I was on in my life. Your kind words of encouragement and constant push have opened my eyes to things that I never thought was possible. Words can't explain how much I appreciate your outlook on things. When I wanted to give up, NOBODY I mean NOBODY, but you were there to push me and to listen to my problems. I thank you so much for that...I love you from the bottom of my heart and always will.

Special thanks go to Michelle Vasquez-Martin. Thanks for introducing me to urban literature. You were the first person to put a five-star read in my hands. If you never would have done that, there's no telling where I would be right now.

Shout outs to Author Kamilah Watson, Author Mika Payne, Author YungLit, Author Terry L. Wroten, Author Envy Red, Author Angel Williams, Author ShaDawne Barner, and Author Author Queen BG, Author/Publisher

Winter Giovanni and Author Tavares "TJ" Jones. Make sure y'all support these authors. Ashanta Obie you're the best Diva…keep those motivational quotes coming. Nene Marie Allen, I have nothing, but love for you. Real recognize real.

Also to everybody that constantly showed me love when that storm came my way. From the phones calls, to the inboxes and the post I received on a daily on my Facebook wall. You all were the one that gave me the strength that I needed to move on. I swear I love each and every one of you (HUGS).

To Tynisha Harvey, I just wanted to say that when that storm came my way, you were there even though you live many miles away. When I woke up crying in the middle of the night, you were there to listen. You checked on me every single day. When I took that 658-mile drive by myself, it was like you were sitting next to me because I talked to you all the way there. So, I just wanted to take the time to say I love you for being the beautiful person that you are.

To my Hustle2Hard team, I love all of y'all…Mi-Mi, R-Ro, Caryn, Pinky, Mesha, and Toya…it's not a party until we step into the building…HA

I can't forget about my CEC family. To everybody that listened to my crazy stories LOL, to the ones that read over my work and to the ones that I joked with on a daily, I have much love for you all. It's just too many of you all to name and I would feel bad if I would have left someone's name out so I played it the safe way LOL.

To the father of my child Derrold "Twin" Davis. I just want to say thank you for giving me a beautiful daughter and continue to stay strong. You and Jerrold are fighters......so all there's left to say is Free "The Twins." To my cuzo Erica, you're here for a reason. You're a fighter. I never met anyone as strong as you. Just remember there is nothing in the world that God and you cannot handle. Love you so much.

To my BFF Todd, I almost forgot about you and I know I wouldn't have heard the last of it. You and I go way back. I mean way back like a sega genesis, like the eight ball leather jacket, like the towel coat, like the gumby haircut...LOL let me stop. Just want to say that I love you and when can I get my money...LOL okay I quit now.

I definitely can't forget these special people that have showed me support in some type of way...Michelle, Karim, Tina, Denise, Kita, Terrinaka, Mercedes, Kyraeki, Tonia, Johnny (the best beautician in the world), thanks for keeping me looking so fly=), Royal Reading book club, My PA family, Melissa Greene-Brown, Shaquan, and Amanda....damn, I know I'm forgetting somebody....SMH

To my cuzo Danielle Latriece Greene, continue to R.I.P. I wish you were here to witness this big accomplishment that I've made. I know you smiling down on me though. I miss you so much.

This is the last shout out then I'm going to let you get to the story...LOL It's only right that I thank my newfound friend, my Editor Brandie Randolph. Just want to say thanks for everything. You're the best.

If I forgot anybody, I'm so sorry; please charge it to my head, not my heart=)

Shoney K

PROLOGUE

*O*ur *Father, which art in heaven, hallowed be thy name. Thy kingdom come, thy will be done on earth as it is in heaven...*

"Bitch, it's too late to pray. The man upstairs can't save you. Nobody can save you. Yo' trifling ass goin' straight to hell, Buttah," Bone stated, viciously.

I regret ever sleeping with him. I guess karma is a motherfucker, but it wasn't supposed to be going down like this. All I remember is Sparkle and I meeting up with this guy at the Ritz Hotel to make a quick $1,000 apiece. Fucking a nigga for money wasn't our main hustle, but we weren't about to pass up that type of money. The average nigga was only willing to pay $500 for some pussy, so when dude offered us that amount, we jumped on it. Once we got to the hotel room, there was no chatting; we instantly started undressing and got down to business. Sparkle began to deep throat him while I rode his face. In the middle of our orgy, the door is kicked in, in comes a man with a mask on his face, with his gun in hand. The first thing that popped in my head was the masked man was there to rob dude, but when he told him to put on his clothes and leave quickly and quietly, my heart dropped to the bottom of my stomach. All I could think about was all the people I've robbed and that the tables had finally turned. If my memory serves correctly, dude came straight toward me and knocked me out with the butt of his gun. The next thing I know, I'm tied to a bedpost being held hostage by this deranged bastard.

I didn't know it was Bone holding me hostage until I was conscious. I tried screaming, but my mouth was taped shut. He noticed me trying to yell, but the only thing he did was laugh while taking off his mask. When I saw his face, I knew that it was the end of the road for me. He was obsessed with me and didn't want to see me with anybody else but him. If he couldn't have me, then no one would.

I glanced around the room to see if the place looked familiar, but it didn't. Fear took over my mind as I began to panic. Still glancing around the room, I noticed that it looked old and reeked of piss. It seemed as if I was in an abandoned attic because when I held my head up, I noticed a window and all I could see was the sky and the top of some trees. I cursed myself repeatedly for sleeping with his psychotic ass.

Several minutes passed before he un-taped my mouth. He sat on the bed rubbing his hand alongside my face. Shaking uncontrollably from fear, I closed my eyes, wishing I was somewhere besides there. Tears began to form in my eyes and trickle down my face. He leaned in toward me, causing me to jump a little, and licked each one of my tears away. He was getting a kick out of being in control.

"Bone, please let me go, pleeeease," I pleaded and begged, repeatedly, until he grabbed me by my neck, cutting my words and breath short. Right before I went unconscious, he let my neck go and I began coughing. More tears began to well up in the corners of my eyes, not from the fear of dying, but from the thought of dying by his hands. I can't believe this is happening to me.

"There's no getting out of this, Buttah. You drove me to this. I love you and this is how you repay me-by sleeping with my brother." *Brother?* I thought to myself. I never slept with his brother. Furthermore, I didn't even know he had a brother. Could the guy at the hotel be his brother? Maybe that's why he just allowed him to put on his clothes to leave. He really had my mind puzzled; but at this point, I didn't even care. All I cared about was being free.

"Bone, please let me go," I pleaded again.

"Hell naw, bitch, you gon' die tonight. You've played with my heart and mind one too many times. I tried to show you how much I love and want to be with you and you couldn't see it 'cause you were too busy being a hoe. I tried giving you the lifestyle that every girl dreams of, but you refused to accept it. Now you leave me no other choice. You don't deserve to live."

When he made that last statement, I began to pray all over again. *Our Father, which art in heaven, hallowed be thy name; thy kingdom come, thy will be done, on earth as it is in heaven...* When Bone heard me starting to pray again, he raised his hand and punched me in my mouth; my lips swelled instantly.

"I told you once, can't no prayer save you! Bitch, I'm your GOD. You were put on this earth to be with me and only me. There are only two ways out of this, Buttah. Either you live happily ever after with me or you die and go to hell and I'll see you when I get there. Take your pick."

I know I did a lot of devious stuff throughout my life, but I didn't deserve the shit that Bone was putting me through. I looked him dead in his eyes and spit in his face. Laughing uncontrollably, Bone wiped the spit from his face and hit me with his pistol. Once again, I was down for the count.

Chapter One
BUTTAH

*E*very bitch and every nigga has a hustle; whether it's a nine-to-five, selling pussy, sucking dick, or selling drugs. Money makes the world go round. Money has always been the ruler of the universe. As Diddy says, *It's all about the Benjamins.* Money is always being made somewhere and somehow. The streets never sleep. Like my brother, J-Boogie, told me, "The game is cold, but it's fair." Every nigga is out to get something, so if that nigga gets his, I'm definitely getting mine. No matter what I have to go through or whose throat I have to cut. I have to come out on top. I have an image to uphold. I'm not your average chick and definitely not that gym shoe-wearing bitch that people are used to seeing. Most bitches hate me because they're not me; it's not my fault they're out here giving that nookie and head up for free. Chicks like that make it hard for a woman like me. Some women have the game fucked up. I know every female has seen the *Player's Club;* they better "use what they got to get what they want" 'cause I'm definitely using what my momma gave me. I have a goldmine between my legs. Pussy is a nigga's weakness. Every man I ever gave my treasure to knows that money makes me cum. I have no shame in my game.

$$\$\$\$\$\$\$\$\$\$$

"Money makes me cum," is the motto that I have chosen to live by. There's no nigga on this earth sticking his third leg in me free. I don't mess around with the average man. To sleep with me, or to even be considered, your profile has to consist of exotic cars, lavish gear, expensive jewelry, and lots of cash. If you don't have all of those qualities, don't look my way. I need a man who is ready and willing to take care of me from the start. I shouldn't have to ask for shit. My expectations are high when it comes to men, simply because I love money and I'm not the average chick. What other explanation do I need?

I stand five-feet, seven, peanut butter complexion, long, silky hair, compliments of my Indian ancestors, chestnut eyes, and a body of a goddess. Not only do I have the looks that men lust after, I have a good head on my shoulders. I attended Clark University and obtained a Bachelor's degree in psychology. I could have easily gotten a job when I graduated, but I chose to take the easy way out. Why work eight or nine hours a day when I can work this pussy for about an hour, if that long, and bring home double of what I would bring home working a full-time job? Working this pussy is what got me this Range Rover and condo overlooking Lake Michigan. I'm only 22 and doing the damn thing. Most men look at me as a hoe or a slut, but who gives a fuck? Not me. Call me what you want because I'm a diva balling out of control on someone else's expense.

$$$$$$$$$

Saturday has finally arrived and all I can think about is hitting the club to see whose pockets I can hit. Ever since Killa, my ex-boo, became state property and will never see the streets again, all I can think about is partying because Killa used to have me on lockdown. Partying for me isn't all about having fun; it's like a job. I scope out the niggas with the deepest pockets, have a conversation with them and if I like what I hear, he's hired. Instead of me paying him, he'll be the one doing the paying. Don't get me wrong, Killa was the love of my life, but life goes on.

Killa and I were together for five years before he was booked. I met him at the tender age of 15. I was still wet behind the ears when it came to men, but boys were something different. Even though I was still play-ing hide-and-go-seek and double Dutch with my friends, I had a fast side to me that only my girl, Honey-bun, knew about.

One boring, rainy day, Honeybun and I went to

the movie theater at North Riverside Mall. When we walked through the door, there he was, standing by the concession stand holding a bag of popcorn in his right hand and a soft drink in his left. He was the finest redbone that I had ever seen. He was dressed in a navy blue and white Rocawear jogging suit with his hat broke to the left and his neck was complimented by an iced out, platinum chain that made him look like he was straight out of a video. I could tell by his demeanor that he was much older than me, but I didn't care. I took off my wet jacket, threw it over my arm, and switched my fast ass over to where he was to start a conversation.

"You look good as hell in that Rocawear jogging suit," I said, smiling from ear to ear.

"Thanks, li'l mama," he said, sucking on his straw to get a taste of his grape pop. He didn't even look my way; he just stood next to the concession stand like he was waiting on someone. I didn't let that discourage me. I liked what I saw, which was *money*, and I wasn't going to let his nonchalant attitude discourage me.

"Nice bling-bling you have around your neck," I said, while smacking on my cherry-flavored Bubblicious. He finally looked in my direction and began to smile. I caught his attention that time.

"I see you are very persistent. How can I help you, li'l momma?"

"Baby boy, this ain't McDonald's, but since you asked, you can help me by givin' me your phone number," I stated jokingly, but I was as serious as a heart attack.

"Shorty, I see you got jokes. How old are you?" He replied, staring straight into my big, chestnut-brown eyes.

"Age ain't nothing but a number and I need seven of yours," I retorted, standing back on my legs as far as they would go with my hands on my hips.

"Young, bold, and beautiful." He managed to get the words out with a smirk on his face. We exchanged numbers and ever since that day, it was me and him against the world, until he was caught slipping. He is now serving two life sentences at Menard Correctional Facility. He was charged with two counts of murder for shooting his best friend, Pete, who was a dirty cop, and his girl, Flame, execution style-all for the love of money. Pete knew that there were two things that Killa hated for a motherfucker to mess with: his money and his girl. Pete chose to violate one of those codes and got fucked. This is the lifestyle I told myself I didn't want to live anymore, but this was the lifestyle that I was accustomed to-bad boys, drug lords, gangsters, and killers. I really do miss him, but, like I said, life goes on.

Since I was accustomed to the finer things in life, I had to make a choice. I had to either find myself a well-paying job or let some street rich nigga take care of me and put up with his bullshit because just about every man comes with baggage. Me being me, I decided to find a street rich nigga because working a job is out of the question.

Chapter Two
HONEYBUN

"Nino, we got a fucking problem," I screamed, throughout our three-bedroom house after slamming the front door.

"I'm upstairs, baby," he stated, in a loud, calm tone.

Stomping up the stairs toward our bedroom, I had the white paper in my hand from the doctor, ready to smack him across the face. This is the second time this year I've contracted an STD from his trifling ass. The first time he gave me gonorrhea and now I have chlamydia. I'm fed up with his cheating ass. When I was diagnosed with gonorrhea and brought it to his attention, we had a big fight and he quickly turned the tables on me, making it seem like I was the one that cheated. If we were presenting our issue in front of the judge, he would have won because his story was convincing. Nino knows I never cheated on him; he just needed something to say because he was caught. Even after he gave me the disease, I remained faithful to him. I should've stop messing with his trifling ass back then.

"Don't 'baby' me, nigga. I see your cheating ass is at it again."

"What you talking about, Honeybun," Nino stated, with a smile on his face. He puckered his lips trying to kiss me, but I quickly turned my head, leaving his kiss to land on air.

"Wipe that fucking smirk off your face. I'm serious. How can I put this so that you can understand the words that are coming out my mouth? Yo' dick is hot; it's on fire again, nigga," I stated, as I threw the paper from the doctor in his face. "Why do you keep doing this to me?"

Avoiding my question, his demeanor changed immediately and he simply stated, "So you been cheating on me again, Honeybun?"

I couldn't believe what I was hearing. This jerk was trying to put it off on me for the second time. "Nino, yo' ass is trifling and I can't deal with your nasty dick ass anymore. It's over, Nino. I swear it's over," I said, between tears. I know the type of guy Nino is, so I should have left the letter from the doctor on the bed, packed my bags and left. I kept my eyes on his hand as I spoke to him because I knew they would be flying in my direction soon.

"First of all, you need to turn that volume down

in your voice and what you mean 'it's over'," he said, and then giggled. "Bitch, where you going? You have no job. Remember, I take care of you," he yelled out and then smacked me.

Holding the side of my face, tears fell freely from my eyes, down my cheeks, landing on my shirt. "Fuck you; I don't need you, Nino. You wrong and you know you wrong."

"Shut the fuck up, Honeybun. Don't say another motherfucking word. I'm about to prove to you I'm not burning."

Grabbing a handful of my hair, Nino dragged me from the entrance of the bedroom door and tossed me on our king-sized bed, causing my head to hit the headboard. Ripping off my shirt, I saw my blue buttons flying in different directions. His tongue fondled my breast as he continued his aggressive behavior by raising my black pencil skirt that hugged my body and spread my legs apart into a perfect split.

"Nino, what the fuck you doing?" I spoke with a distraught look on my face.

Punching me in my mouth without hesitation, he spoke, "Didn't I just tell you to shut the fuck up?" I instantly felt the swelling of my upper lip.

Not saying another word, I lay there with tears rolling down my face. Nino and I fought quite often, but it never led to him raping me. Nino jammed his infected dick into my infected pussy. He began humping me like a stray dog. I couldn't believe what he was doing. He has really lost his mind. I can't continue to deal with Nino. Enough is enough.

With every hump, he spoke, "Do you think if I had chlamydia, my dick would be able to perform like this? This dick is too good to be burning. This is a disease free dick. Now tell daddy this is the best dick you ever had."

I continued laying there, not saying a word, and contemplating my next move.

"Bitch, I know you hear daddy talking to you. Now tell me what I want to hear. Is this dick the best you ever had?"

First, the nigga don't want me to say anything, now he wants me to talk. He needs to make his fucking mind up. Mumbling, I answered, "Yeah, this is the best dick I ever had."

"I can't hear you, baby, a li'l louder," he said, breathing heavily as he continued to hump me.

"Yes, baby, it's the best I ever had."

Easing himself out of me, he yelled out, "Now turn over for me, baby! I don't want to see nothing but ass."

He has to be kidding me. He knows how much I hate anal sex. I continued to lie on my back. I refuse to let him stick his big manhood inside of my ass. Anal sex was something that I just couldn't get with. The feeling was so uncomfortable for me. He saw that I wasn't moving, so he wrapped his hands around my neck and with a firm grip, he looked deeply into my eyes. As I stared back into his demonic looking eyes, I saw a combination of love and hate staring back at me.

My thoughts were interrupted when I felt a sharp pain shoot through my body. Nino had entered my ass while I laid flat on my back. I screamed out in pain. I tried to push away from him, but his firm grip around my neck wouldn't allow me to go anywhere. Moments later, his grip loosened from around my neck and he fell on top of me.

Nino had me terrified at this point. He was really tripping, but despite what he just done to me, I built up enough courage to tell him, "I'm still leaving your sorry ass, nigga."

"Wait a minute. Wait a minute. Calm down, baby," he stated, as he rubbed his hand alongside my face.

Here he goes with his bipolar ass ways. One minute, he acts like a loving significant other and the next, he treats me like the bottom of his shoe by physically and mentally abusing me.

"Wait a minute, my ass. It's over." Deep in my heart, I didn't want to leave him because I was accustomed to the lifestyle that he provided for me, but if I stayed, I knew one of two things was going to happen. Either I kill him or be killed. Nino had me scared of him, but if I showed fear, he would continue to walk over me.

"We both are overreacting, baby. I got upset because you accused me of cheating and giving you a disease. I love you too much to do that and you know

23

that, girl. You're not going anywhere because I need you."

"Nino, how am I overreacting you cheated on me, gave me a STD, then turn around and raped me."

"Baby, I just told you I never cheated on you," he said, persuasively, "and how can I rape my own woman? Be for real, Honeybun."

"Woman or not, you just raped me and if you never cheated, then why in the hell am I walking around with chlamydia? Please tell me 'cause I know I never cheated on you," I shouted.

"Baby, listen, maybe when you used those public bathrooms you contracted the STD."

Laughing aloud, but seriously, I replied to his stupid remark, "You got to be kidding me. It's whatever, Nino; just go get treated."

As I got off the bed, Nino stood up, wrapped his arms around me and kissed me gently on my forehead as my arms hung freely, not wanting to touch him. Being in his arms has become an awkward feeling over the last couple of months. The love that I have for him is slowly fading. When I first met Nino, he was such a sweetheart. He gave me the utmost respect. He never called me out of my name and he never put his huge hands on me. I wished he still possessed the same qualities.

"Nino, I gotta go. I need some air and plus, I need to go get this prescription filled. I'll be back in a li'l bit," I spoke, as I eased my way from his arms.

"Okay, baby, but I might be gone when you get back, though. I got a li'l business I need to go handle."

Business, I hope his business consists of going to the doctor and finding the trick that burnt him, I thought.

After I jumped out of the shower and got dressed, I grabbed my purse off the doorknob and headed out the door with a million and one things on my mind. I took a quick walk around the block to try to clear my head before I got in the car, but that didn't work.

Relaxing under AC, I thought about all the bull-shit I've been through when it came to dealing with Nino. I can remember one particular incident when I was at the beauty shop being dazzled up for my girl, Buttah's, birthday party at the W Hotel. I was sitting in the chair getting my hair whipped up talking to my beautician, Angie, when we heard the sound of car windows being broken. I was never the nosey type, but Angie was the total opposite. She ran her 250-pound body frame to the window and said in her ghetto tone, "I know whoeva windows those is gonna be mad as hell."

Sometimes, Angie could be too damn nosey for me. My patience was running short with her, so I yelled out, "Get yo' ass back over here and finish my hair so I can get up out of here. I got shit to do, Angie, damn!"

"Wait a minute, girl. The chick is still out here; she cutting the tires now. This bitch has lost her damn mind. Girl, you need to see this. Hold up one minute. You need to get over here 'cause that looks like yo' car."

I jumped from my seat with a half done head and ran out the door as fast as I could. When I got outside, I was beyond pissed; the bitch had busted three of my windows out and put all four of my tires on flat. The blonde, ghetto-looking chick jumped in her car as soon as she saw me run out of the shop. I knew this incident had to involve Nino's trifling ass in some way. The girl pulled off quickly and yelled out the window, "Stay the fuck away from Nino. He's my man. It's because of you he's neglecting my child." I was shocked by that comment because he has only one baby's momma to my knowledge and she was not her. I could do nothing but stand there in disgust and think of what I was going to do to Ms. Blondie once I found out who she was. I took a mental picture of her face and promised to give her an ass beating that she would never forget.

$$SSSSSSSSS$$

Still en route, I skipped passed the pharmacist and headed straight to the mall. I didn't care if my lip was swollen. I needed to clear my mind and shopping is the only remedy for me. Looking at my watch and realizing the time, I smashed my foot on the gas pedal because my home girl, Ladybug, was at work, so that meant I didn't have to pay full price for some of the items I purchase from Bloomingdales.

Hitting just about every store in the mall, I

smiled because the lighter my pockets became, the happier I became. It didn't take me long to spend the 2,000 dollars that was in my pocket. I was in and out the mall in about two hours; that was definitely a record for me.

"Excuse me," I spoke to the young woman as I approached my car.

"Oh, my fault. Let me get out your way," the girl spoke, as she dusted off one of her knees. "My keys had fallen and landed under your car," she spoke, in a pleasant tone.

"Don't I know you from someone," I stated, as I continued to stare closely at the girl.

"Ummm...ummm...I don't think so."

"I swear, you look so familiar. I just can't put my finger on it right now. I know as soon as I get in my car and drive down the street, it will come to me. Well, enjoy your day."

"You do the same," she spoke.

As I loaded the Bloomingdale's and bebe bags into my car, I carried on with my day. I dreaded going back to that house with Nino. I didn't want to see his face any time soon, but I didn't want to be seen outside by anyone else with my swollen lip, either. The next stop was the pharmacist to drop off my prescription.

I was only in the drug store 10 minutes before I ran back to my car. As I ran my hand alongside my door, my heart ached. I loved my SLK Mercedes Benz convertible. I couldn't believe what I was seeing. As my fingers traced the words 'Stupid Bitch' that was engraved into my candied-apple red paint job, I was furious. I ran to the crowd of people that was standing on the corner and asked if they saw anybody near my car and they said no. The streets were crowded as usual for a day in June, so I knew that whoever did this wasn't bold enough to do this on a busy main street. Then it hit me like a ton of bricks. My mind quickly went back to the mall. I knew that girl looked familiar. She was the same girl that vandalized my car while I was at the beauty shop. I didn't recognize her because Ms. Blondie was now Ms. Blackie. She had a different color weave in her hair.

I should have known that something wasn't right when she said she was picking up her keys and I didn't see any keys in her hand. What I saw was a small sharp object, but blew it off because I had other things on my mind.

$$\mathcal{SSSSSSSS}$$

Pulling into the driveway of my house, I was beyond pissed and I blamed Nino for everything. I got out the car, slammed the door, and shook my head while staring at the neatly engraved words. Full of rage, all that crossed my mind was hurting the bitch that did the damage to my car. There is no way I'm going to let her get away with this.

First slamming the screen door, then the main door to the house, I began to call Nino's name.

"Nino, Nino!" There was no response.

I called his name again, but there was still no answer. I remembered that he told me that he might be gone once I got back. He must have jumped in the car with one of his friends because his car was still in the driveway.

Sitting on the living room couch, I thought about my car. I'm appalled behind this. What gave this girl the audacity to fuck with my car? Once again, I blamed Nino. If he learns to keep his dick in his pants, I wouldn't be going through this.

"Nino," I yelled out again, and stormed from room to room looking for him in hopes he is here.

Catching my attention, I heard music coming from upstairs; it was cut down low, almost as if the singer was whispering from where I was standing from. The music led me to our bedroom. As I got closer to the room, I peeked in and noticed he wasn't there. I walked down the hall to the first guestroom and still, there was no Nino. I continued to the second guestroom and was stopped in my tracks when I heard sexual moans. Instantly, an image of me murdering him went through my mind. Today is the day I would send him to meet his maker. I know he doesn't have some hoe in our house. I know he's not that crazy. I hope he's not that crazy. I quickly ran into our bedroom and grabbed my gun from underneath the bed that he gave to me for Christmas the first year we were together. That alone should've told me the type of person he was, but I didn't care. I needed a thug in my life and I guess every thug needs a couple of ladies because he can't be a one woman's man if his life depended on it. If he has a hoe in our house, I'm going to shoot them both. I tiptoed out of the bedroom and headed toward the guestroom. Before I got to the room, I stopped because I didn't hear the moans anymore. Was my mind playing tricks on me? I went into the room and didn't see a soul in sight. *Damn, where the hell did they go?* As if on cue, I heard the moans all over again and they became clearer and more intense. They were coming from the guest bathroom. I had Black, that's the name of my gun, in my hand, ready to shoot any naked body moving. The bathroom door was cracked just enough so I could see what was going on. When I peeked inside, what I saw before my eyes took me by surprise. Nino was sitting his stanking ass on the edge of the bathtub with his pants dropped to his ankles. He had his eyes closed with his phone to his ear and his dick in his hand jacking off. The nigga was having phone sex. He can get pussy from me anytime, but he'd rather have phone sex with some bitch. I was devastated. I didn't say anything. As bad as it hurt me, I just stood by the door with tears running down my face and listened to his perverted ass.

"Tell me how you want it," he said, as he moaned softly. "Whose it is? Call me daddy. I like it when you call me Big Poppa." Enough was enough. I just walked away quietly, headed out the front door, and made a mental note to myself to go back to my old ways. From this day forward, it's all about me.

Chapter Three
SPARKLE

M r. Rodgers always said, "It's a beautiful day in the neighborhood." I wonder what neighborhood he grew up in; definitely not mine. My neighborhood consisted of crack-heads, child molesters, hoes, and killers. Not a white picket fence, a dog, and loving parents. This type of shit was only seen on TV where I'm from. I grew up on the west side of Chicago, one of the toughest sides in the city, and there were no white picket fences in sight. My life was a living hell up until the age of 16 when I was able to think for myself. Life before then was not peaches and cream.

At the age of 10, the hoe that gave birth to me took away my pride and dignity. She allowed just about every man in our neighborhood to invade my young temple just so she could get high. I know we are not supposed to disrespect our parents, but what mother would sale her precious daughter's body for drugs? I hate her so much for that. Even though this happened years ago, it's still fresh in my mind.

The first man my mother allowed to invade my space was Sam. He was an Arab that owned the liquor store three blocks away from our run down roach invested apartment. He was short and fat. His belly was the biggest thing on his body. He smelled like he never took a shower or a bath. Sam and my mother had become quite close over the course of the years we lived in the drug-infested neighborhood. He knew that she had a bad drug habit and he used that to his advantage. My mom would have sex with him for her drug money, and for whatever she needed out his store.

One hot muggy day, my mom and I walked into Sam's liquor store. She picked up a 22-ounce bottle of Old English, placed it on the counter, and asked Sam for a pack of Newport 100s.

He rung her up and said, "$8." She looked at him like he was crazy.

He gave her the same look in return and stated, "Not this time."

"What do you mean? What do I have to do? I'll suck your dick, man. It's only $8."

Sam was getting tired of my mom because she was worn out. She looked like the female version of Smokey from *New Jack City.* She wasn't the pretty Stacy she used to be back in the day. The drugs had taken total control over her and her appearance. It affected everything that she did. Drugs were her life and nothing else mattered to her, not even me.

Sam shook his head from left to right to indicate that he wasn't going to give her anything. He looked at me and winked his left eye. My mom noticed him staring. She begins to look at me with a devious smile upon her face as if a light bulb came on in her head. She then glanced back to Sam's horrible smelling ass and asked him "Do you want her." I couldn't believe what I was hearing. I know that drugs fuck with your mind, but damn sale your daughter just to get a fix.

"I will have her to suck your dick for $100, a 22-ounce of Old English, and a pack of cigarettes." His smelly ass had the nerve to smile. At the age of ten was the first time I had a piece of spoiled meat in my mouth.

Sam closed the store for approximately thirty minutes. He grabbed me by my hand and led me to the back of his store. He told me to get on my knees. I obeyed like an obedient child should with no complaints. He then proceeded to pull out his two-inch penis with his ashy hands. My whole body felt numb. I couldn't believe my mom was going to allow this to happen. I started crying uncontrollably. He grabbed a hand full of my hair very tight and pushed my head toward his penis. I tried to pry his hand from my hair, but couldn't. He looked at my mom who was standing behind me and said "if you want this money within the next three minutes she better be sucking my dick 'cause I have a store to run." My mom looked at me with shame in her eyes, but still yelled out, "Look, li'l heffa, Momma needs this money, so put his dick in your mouth so we can go. I don't have all day. He doesn't have all day. He has a business to run." Still crying uncontrollably, I grabbed Sam's two-inch penis and stuck it in my mouth. I had the slightest idea as to what I was doing. Hell, I was only ten years old, still playing with Barbie dolls. I'd seen this done on TV before, but still, I had no clue as to what I was doing. Sam tried coaching me through it, but I wasn't paying him any attention. I just wanted to get this over with.

Twenty minutes later, I was still down on my knees when I began to feel his hand get tighter around my ponytails and his knees began to bulk. Next thing I know white shit was all over my face. At the time, I didn't know what was going on. I made the old bastard nut. It was finally over with and he was satisfied, and so was my mom. Since that unpleasant incident, my mom used my body to get what she wanted from all the men in our neighborhood.

After my mom exposed me to all those men, I became comfortable with what I was doing and I became her personal assistant. She gave me one on one session's on how to please a man and how to get in their pockets. Once I mastered how to please a man, I help my mom out with some of the bills. You would think my mom was ashamed of what she was making me do, but as long as we got our bills paid and she had drugs in her system nothing else mattered to her. It was to the point that she was running a mother and daughter whorehouse. Like I said, I learned from the best. I was very observant when it came to pleasing a man. I watched and learned quickly. On several occasions, my mom would have the landlord in her bedroom giving him some "sent from heaven" type of loving so we wouldn't have to pay rent for the next couple of months. I would peek through the hole in my bedroom closet, which my mom made for me, that leads to her bedroom and watched her perform on the old man like she was a porn star. Sometimes, she didn't need to have sex with the men that came in and out of our house because her mouthpiece was dangerous. The game that came out her mouth was vicious. You would have thought she had a couple of whores on the corner of Cicero and Roosevelt with the game she would spit at those men. Crack-head or not, my mom knew how to handle business. "It's all about the mouth piece," is what she would say once her tricks left our apartment. I learned the thing with winning any man over is to tell them what they want to hear, do as they say, never talk back, and let them believe they own the pussy." The pussy is a powerful weapon, and with the type of weapon I'm working with, I can't lose.

$$$$$$$$

Now, I can agree with Mr. Rodgers, there is definitely a beautiful day in the neighborhood. I have my own crib, my own car, no kids, no man, and plenty of tricks. My mom used my body to get what she wanted; I might as well do the same so thanks to her tricking niggas out of money really came easy for me. I will admit I have a messed up way of thinking and I blame my mom for that, but what she has taught me has prepare me on how to survive on my own. I will also admit that my sex drive is out of control. I have sex morning, noon, and night. "Sex Me, Baby" is my first, middle, and last name. I have no sexual preference. I look at myself as a tri-sexual, meaning I'm willing to "try" anything when it comes to sex whether it's with a man or a woman as long as the price is right. I don't care what color or size you are; as long as you have dead presidents in your pocket, we can do whatever.

My first experience with a woman was about three years ago, and she blew my mind. I met her through a good friend of mine named Marcus. I was tricking off with him for $500 when he came to me with a proposal. Marcus' sex game was off the chain. He just didn't know that I would have given him the cat free if he wanted it because his sex was just that good. While lying in bed with Marcus, he rubbed his hands up and down my thick thighs and he asked me in a tone that was almost a whisper, "Have you ever been with a woman?" and I told him "No." Sleeping with a woman never crossed my mind. What can a woman do for me? I thought to myself. Marcus told me he would give me an extra $250 if I allowed him to bring a woman in the bed with us. The extra money sounded good, but I couldn't fathom me being with nobody other than a man. I was terrified. No man has ever asked me that question before. Was I ready for this? Could I live with myself knowing that I might enjoy another woman touching me? Would I be a lesbian? All types of questions started running through my mind, but in the end, I agreed to do what Marcus wanted because money talks and bullshit walks.

He must've had her on speed dial because 15 minutes later, a tall beautiful woman walked into the room. She had on a tan three quarter length trench coat that was tied tightly around her small waist. Taking off her coat, I noticed her skin was flawless. Her body was the prettiest peanut butter complexion that I had ever seen. She was wearing a brown thong with a matching bra that complimented her skin, with a pair of gold pumps. The woman was breathtaking. I thought I was beautiful. This woman had it going on. She didn't have one scar on her body. There was a small tattoo of a strawberry on her stomach that made me want to lick all over it. I must admit, I was infatuated by how well her body was put together. She had me second-guess my sexual preference; she definitely turned me on. Just looking at her made my nipples get hard and my pussy get wet. Marcus introduced us to each other. He told Buttah that this was my first time and to be gentle. She giggled a little and walked toward me. She reached for my left hand and placed it into her right hand. She pulled me off the bed pulling me closer to her and whispered in my ear "just relax." Her voice was so peaceful and genuine. The way she talked to me made me feel so comfortable. She gently pushed me back down on the king sized bed and ran her fingers up and down the curves of my naked body. I welcomed her touch even though I was nervous as hell. Marcus saw the nervousness in my eye and walked toward me. He kissed me on my lips gently and told me to go with the flow. Buttah made her way to my private area and slid her index and middle fingers inside of me. Moving her fingers in and out of me, I moaned. She smiled. She began to lick her finger one by one tasting my juices. She then proceeded to let her tongue walk up and down my body. Her tongue was extra moist. When she reached the core of my apple, she took me to ecstasy. She sucked this pussy like she does this on a regular basis. She did it better than Marcus. Marcus was enjoying watching her please me. From the corner of my eyes, I watched him place his dick in his hand, moving it up and down very slowly while moaning, "Suck that pussy, girl." I was so into it. I couldn't believe I was enjoying myself. I didn't know what had gotten into me, but I pulled Buttah's head from between my legs and pushed her down onto the bed. I spread her legs like an eagle would do his wings and put my tongue to work. I spread her pussy lips apart and let my tongue do the talking. I moved my head in a circular motion until I heard her moan in pleasure. She was moaning like crazy. I'm glad she was enjoying herself because this was my first time.

While giving her head, Marcus walked behind me and entered me from behind. His penis felt so good inside of me. I never experienced sexual pleasure like that before. The type of energy that was in that room had me so I high I never wanted to come down. For the next hour and a half, the three of us had sex like wild animals. Afterward, we all lay in bed together because we were exhausted from all that sexual healing. Just like a typical man after sex, Marcus smoked a cigarette and fell asleep. While Buttah and I lay in bed, we got to know one another. We found out that we had a lot in common and the main thing was the love for money. We exchanged phone numbers and became good friends. Even though we had a good time with each other that night, we never had sex with each other again. That night was all about business.

$$\$\$\$\$\$\$\$\$\$$

"Where the fuck is he; time is of the essence. I need to get to the mall before it closes." I shouted while staring out the window. I need to pick up a pair of Chanel pumps because Buttah, Honeybun, I were going men hunting tonight. At least Buttah and I are because Honeybun is too in love with her man to do anything. Something told me to get the money from his stupid ass last night. It's my fault giving that nigga pussy on credit. The sex is the bomb, but I still need to be paid. I could call one of my other tricks, but for what he's the one that let the cat out of the bag.

I met Bone two Friday's ago at a reggae club. The brother caught my eye after a couple of drinks. I hoped the drinks weren't playing tricks with my mind because the boy was fine. He wore shoulder-length dreads, stood 6'5", bow-legged, Hershey chocolate complexion, deep dimples, and had a body like the guy that gave Stella her groove back. Bone was on the dance floor rolling his body on some chicken-head to one of Sean Paul's songs. The way he was rolling, I knew he could fuck. I wanted him and I was going to get him. I wanted him to roll all over this five foot four inch body frame of thickness that I have. From the looks of it, he didn't have one flaw, but I know that looks can be deceiving. He was iced out in all the right places, and he was dressed to impress. When he got off the dance floor, he went straight to the bar. I unbuttoned my top button on my Chanel mini dress that showed off my thick legs, and pranced over to where he was. Our eyes connected instantly.

I never was the shy type, so I introduced myself. "Hi, I'm Sparkle," I said, in my most seductive voice. He looked at me from head to toe and his soldier stood to full attention. I always have that type of effect on men when I came within inches from them. He extended his right hand toward mine, nails freshly manicured, and grabbed my hand. He guided my hand to his lips, placed four gentle kisses on it, and twirled me around. I guess he wanted to get a good look at what I had to offer. There was an instant sexual attraction between us. I felt a tingling sensation run through my body. We stayed at the bar for a while and he bought me a couple of drinks. We chatted getting to know one another, then danced. We chatted some more, drunk some more, then fucked. Yea I said it; we fucked right in the ladies washroom. The best dick I ever had in my 20 years. As we were leaving out the ladies room, he whispered in my ear, "By the way, my name is Bone." This is how I ended up in the predicament I'm in now, dick whipped. I definitely need to have more dick control. The messed up part about everything is all the lovemaking we've been doing over the course of the weeks, I finally realize he isn't a major player in the league. Don't get me wrong he gives me money, but it's never a large amount at one time. It's a hundred dollars or two maybe every week and that's a strong maybe.

Still looking out the window like a sad puppy, I saw Bone turn the corner finally thirty-five minutes later, leaving me with only one and half hours to shop. He doubled parked his car and got out with a smirk on his face. Before he got a chance to get to the porch, there I was standing with my arms folded. He knew that I was upset. He didn't say a word. He handed me the money kissed me on the forehead and left.

Chapter Four
BUTTAH

I left my condo a little past 11:30 p.m. to pick up Sparkle and Honeybun so we could head to the club. I was dressed in my blue jean bebe jumpsuit with my four-inch Gucci pumps and matching Gucci handbag. I jumped on interstate 290, headed westbound, and blasted T.I.'s song, *Whatever You Like*. The lyrics gave me motivation.

Shawty, you the hottest, love the way you drop it, brain
so good coulda swore you went to college,
100k deposit, vacation in the tropic,
everybody knows it ain't tricking if you got it.

If a nigga isn't on what TI is on, they can keep it moving. I pulled my blunt from my ashtray and lit it. I took one good pull and started choking. "This is some good ass weed," I spoke aloud, as if someone was sitting next to me. The weed had me floating on cloud nine. I put my foot to the pedal and within 15 minutes, I was pulling in front of Sparkle's house. I pulled out my blackberry, turned down my radio, and then proceeded to dial her seven digits. The phone rang three times before she picked up.

"I'm downstairs," I yelled into the phone.

"Here I come," she replied.

Waiting patiently for Sparkle to come out the house, I continued to bob my head to TI's song. After waiting 10 minutes, she decided to walk out her front door. I was a little frustrated when she got downstairs because I hate waiting on anybody. I'm an on time person and I expect everybody to be one too especially when dealing with me. When a bitch is on my time, they need to act like Speedy Gonzalez. If it wasn't for my blunt that had me calm, I would have went haywire on her ass. My thought process changed immediately when I saw Bone sexy ass on her arm. She kissed him and they went their separate ways. Damn he's fine, I said softly to myself, but his money isn't long enough for me. According to Sparkle, the only thing he has good going for himself is sex. If he had deep pockets, he would be able to tap this ass at any given time.

Personally, I feel there are certain things that you should never tell *any* woman. I don't care if she's your mother, sister, cousin, aunt, and especially your friends. The main thing is to never, ever, ever tell them about your sex life because bitches are scandalous. They will sleep with your man behind your back, laugh, and giggle in your face. The reason I know is that I'm one of those scandalous bitches. I have sex for money with no strings attached. I don't care about the next female's feelings because I have bills that need to be paid. I try not to have sex with my friend's man, but sometimes things just happen. I slept with three of Sparkle's men and one of Honeybun's. I felt bad afterward, but my pockets were fatter.

"What's up, girl," I asked Sparkle, while staring at Bone as he walked to his car. I couldn't keep my eyes off him. It's something about a man with dreads that turns me on. Even though he's below my standards, I might just have to try him. If I decide to give Bone a taste of my goodies, it really wouldn't be about the money, of course, he would have to give up something, and all I really want to know is he all what Sparkle says he is.

"Nothing at all, I'm just ready to go to the club to get my party on."

"I feel you on that. I see you and Bone are still kicking it." I wasn't concerned. I was just being nosy. It really didn't matter if they were together or not because her being with him was not going to stop me from fucking him if I wanted to.

"I guess you can say that, I just can't stop messing with him. He knows how to put it down on a sista. Enough about him, let's just go to the club, so I can find Mr. Richie Rich."

"I feel you, girl. There's nothing wrong with

that. Looking for Mr. Richie Rich is the number one thing on our agenda tonight."

"Have you spoken with Honeybun?" Sparkle asked changing the subject.

"Yep, I spoke with her briefly. I told her slow ass she better run down the stairs as soon as she hear my horn 'cause if she don't, she will be driving herself."

"I heard that girl. Honeybun is slow as hell. It always takes her 'bout two hours to get dressed. I haven't the slightest idea as to what she's trying to do to herself 'cause if ya got it, ya got it. If ya don't, ya don't."

Sparkle and Honeybun can't stand each other because of my brother J-Boogie, but tolerate each other because of me. They both use to date him at the same time. It wasn't my business, or place to tell them they both were sleeping with him. Hell, blood is thicker than water. Honeybun felt I was obligated to tell her because I knew her longer than Sparkle. Hell, he's a man and there's one thing that all females should know about men, they all are dogs, some are just trained better than others. Honeybun is the one who has the problem with Sparkle because J-Boogie chose Sparkle over her. He told me that he chose Sparkle because her pussy tastes better. I couldn't do anything, but laugh because he wasn't telling me anything that I didn't know. Sparkle does taste like candy.

"When I spoke to Honeybun she mentioned that she is ready to leave Nino's cheating butt. She caught him in the bathroom with his dick in his hand, literally having phone sex," I laughed, while explaining to Sparkle.

"Girl, that's some shit for ya. She should've left him a long time ago. I told her before she got in too deep that he wasn't shit. He's a dog ass nigga. I guess she's still bitter at me about your brother and she doesn't want to believe nothing I have to say."

"Like I told her, it's his loss, not hers."

"What make this time so different from the other times? She always says she's going to leave him and never does."

"I don't know, but a woman can only take and go through so much with a man before she washes her hands." I said with an attitude, but not directed toward anybody in particular. Honeybun is my girl and she shouldn't have to go through the stuff she's going through with him. I never knew what she saw in him in the first place.

"You and I both know what she see in him, so stop playing stupid. It's all the Benjamins, baby," Sparkle said, in between laughs.

As soon as I was about to honk the horn, Honeybun came running out the door. I guess she was sitting in the window watching out for me.

"Hey," she said, drily.

"Girl, cheer up," I said, and reached toward the back seat to give her a hug. She glanced at Sparkle and spoke to her. I can tell that she is getting over that J-Boogie shit. Hell, she should have been over that shit, it happened almost two years ago.

Before pulling off, I reached underneath my seat and retrieved my CD case. I flipped through a couple of pages until I came across the perfect CD to boost up each one of our self-esteem, not that we need any because we all were fly. I popped in Trina's CD and blasted *Da Baddest Bitch.* I put my feet to the pedal once again, jumped on interstate 290, and headed eastbound to the club.

When the song ended, I turned the speakers down and yelled out, "Ladies, I hit a lick a couple of nights ago. I've been scoping this nigga out from up north. At first, he was trying to play hard to get, but it wasn't long before I wheeled him in. After I gave him a sneak peek of my assets, he couldn't resist this body. No lie; this was the easiest $2,000 that I've ever made in my life. First, I laid the pussy down and the only reason why I did that was that he was Morris Chestnut fine. Right after we had sex, we relaxed a little and I fixed him a triple shot of Grey Goose. When he had his head turned, I slipped three dorms sleeping capsules in his drink. He drank the Goose like it was water and instantly the mixture of the alcohol and sleeping pills went into his system taking full affect causing him to fall into a deep sleep instantly. I enjoyed every moment of robbing his little-dicked ass. I would have gone easy on his pockets if he wasn't trying to play a sister in the beginning and plus the sex wasn't all that. I took my time putting back on my clothes because I knew he wasn't waking up any time soon. I even ordered room service and ate a meal before I left. I know when he woke up he was pissed off. The only thing I left in his pocket was ten dollars and the reason I did that was to make sure he had gas money to get home. I guess I do have a heart after all." I said chuckling to myself. "These niggas don't give two flying fucks about me, so why should I care about them. It's a mean world and we all live in it."

"You got that right," Honeybun said. "Fuck these niggas they ain't on shit."

"So tonight everything is on me. I'm a make it rain. Everybody is going to hate on us like always." I love to stunt when I go out. You can call me the "Number One Stunna."

"Make sure you make it pour down," Sparkle said, then high fived Honeybun.

When we pulled up to the club, the line was around the corner. By me being me, I valet parked my purple Range, jumped out, and me and my girls strutted our fine asses straight to the front door looking like America's Next Top Models. We were dressed to the "T" from head to toe. All eyes were on us as we walked by. The niggas were holding their dicks wondering what it would feel like to be with one of us and the females were rolling their eyes as we walked pass them wishing they were us. We were stopped in our tracks when we reached the door by this oversized bouncer.

"Ladies, the line is around the corner," he said,

while pointing his index finger at me.

I looked at him like he was stupid. He must don't know who he's talking to. I don't do lines especially when I'm sleeping with the owner of the club.

"I know the line is around the corner, that's why we are here and not back there," I stated as I pointed my finger in his face.

"Ladies I need..." I put my hand up to cut him off in mid-sentence. My baby, Dee, was exiting the club and I yelled out his name.

"Hey, baby," he said, as he gave me a kiss on my cheek looking sexy as hell dressed in an all-white linen suit.

"Can you tell your new bouncer that he needs to learn me and my girl's faces and also let him know that we don't pay to get in your club nor do we stand in line?"

He looked at dude and told him, "You heard the lady, they don't pay to get in, nor do they stand in line." I just smiled at dude's oversized ass and walked straight through the double doors.

As soon as we walked through the door, we heard the DJ doing his thing. He was playing *Mrs. Officer* by Lil Wayne. All the 'hood niggas were feeling that song. You could see everyone's lips moving saying they wanted to "Rodney King a bitch."

Just about everybody in the club knew who we were. As we walked through the crowd the broke men were pulling at our hands trying to get our attention, but we didn't give them the time of day. We headed straight to the VIP section and I ordered a bottle of Moet. That's Honeybun's favorite drink and I knew that she needed to get her drink on so she could get her mind off Nino. I also ordered each one of us a Pretty Girl. I really didn't have to pay for anything in the club because of the affiliation I have with Dee, but I felt I should give him back a couple of the dollars that he gives me on a daily basis. I didn't feel like I was missing any money because it was recycled right back into my pockets.

The club was packed to capacity as usual and there were many illegal transactions going on. They had pussy for sale in the green room, grams of cocaine in the blue room, and pills and weed behind the bar. If I were the police, I would have made head detective that night.

All the major hustlers where out. Normally when we go out it be five females to one man, but for some particular reason this night the role was reversed. Fat, skinny, short, tall, ugly, or fine, I didn't care; as long as their wallets were fat, they could have my attention.

Upon scanning the room, I noticed Dough-Boy on the other side sitting with his fan club. All the females were crazy about him including me, and I was determined to be the main woman in his life. He was the Bill Gates of Chicago. He was one of those 'round the way' guys that every nigga knew and wanted to be and every female wanted. He was the leader of his own organization called MAT (Money Ain't a Thang). Those boys were being paid and I was determined to be the first lady. I have no problem with approaching a man, but I didn't want to seem thirsty. When you approach a man like him, you have to be on your square at all times so I definitely had to come up with a game plan to get him.

Chapter Five
HONEYBUN

I'm so glad I decided to go out. A whole week flew by since the incident took place with me and Nino. If I would have stayed in the house and looked at him for another minute, I was going to catch a case. I really needed to clear my head and hanging with my girls was definitely the answer. It was time that I started thinking about me and put Nino on the back burner. I'm far from ugly and it was time that I explore my options.

I was having a good time with this one guy. He was average looking, but he had my undivided attention. He stood about 5'7", short fade, with chocolate chip colored eyes. As I stood at the bar laughing and talking to him I noticed Nino walking through the door. "Damn," I said aloud, but dude didn't hear me because he was ordering me another drink. This nigga is always trying to spoil my fun. I looked at dude and told him "I'll be right back." He didn't know it, but I had no intention of coming back because I was worried about what Nino would do to us if he saw us talking. I headed back to the table to inform my girls that Nino's crazy ass was there.

Upon me and my girl enjoying our drinks, Nino approached our table and told me to go home. I looked at him like he was stupid. I wasn't going anywhere. I was out with my girls trying to have a good time and I wasn't going to let him ruin that under any circumstances.

"Nino, I'm not going anywhere." I said with a matter-of-fact attitude. My drink was definitely kicking in because under normal circumstances, I would never have fixed my mouth to talk back to him in public because I know the consequences that comes alone with that.

"Honeybun, I'm only going to tell your ass one more time. Get your things and leave and if you don't, I'm going to drag your ass up out of here."

"You are not going to touch her while we're standing right here," Buttah vented out.

"This don't have anything to do with you or Sparkle, so get out my fuckin' business. If I tell her she has to leave, she's leaving. I don't even know why I allow her to hang out with you two sluts anyway, but as of today she's not."

"Nigga, you ain't her daddy. You can't tell her

who the fuck she can hang out with. She's a grown ass woman," Sparkle said, getting in on the conversation.

"I am her daddy and if you want, I can be your daddy too," Nino stated, as he admired Sparkle's body.

"Nino, you so damn disrespectful, I'll be a fool to leave with you."

"So what are you saying," he stated while walking closer to me, but before I got a chance to answer his question he smack the shit out of me. I went flying directly to the ground. My face was burning. It felt like he smacked me with a ball of fire. Tears instantly formed in the wells of my eyes. It wasn't because he smacked me that had me about to cry it was because of the humiliation I just received in front of the big as crowd at the party.

As if on cue, Buttah and Sparkle rushed him. That's just how my girls and I got down. If one of us is down on the ground, we all fought no matter who it is. Buttah grabbed a corona bottle from somebody's table getting ready to split his head to the white meat, but before she had a chance to do that, one of his guys intervene pushing her directly on the ground. Sparkle jumped on the guy's back that had pushed Buttah and seconds later Buttah was back on her feet joining in the fight. We all know there's no comparison between a woman's strength and a man's strength, but we didn't care. We were determined to make an example out of them. We weren't scared to fight a man because most men are bitches as niggas anyway.

Security finally came over to where we were and broke up the commotion. He directed his attention right to Buttah and asked her if she was all right. She told him yes. Security told Nino that he had to leave the party, but Nino wasn't having it. Nino is far from a punk, he's not just a woman beater he'll beat a nigga ass in a minute. He stood his ground and after a brief conversation with the bouncer, he smiled, but before walking away, he yelled out, "I came out for a couple of drinks to clear my head and I'll be damn if I let you three fuck that up. I'm just gonna let you hoes be." He walked away very quickly and vanished into the crowd.

Once we regained our composure, we went back to partying like nothing ever happened. "That's my song," I said while jumping out my seat and running to the dance floor. Whether Nino was there or not, I was going to continue to have a good time. I was on the dance floor dropping it like it hot when I noticed a red-haired chick watching me from the bar. Instantly, I recognized the face. Her hair color wasn't going to fool me this time. Even though I'm tipsy, I knew what I was seeing was accurate. This is the same bitch that busted out my car windows, flattened, my tires, and engraved stupid bitch on my car door. My mind wasn't playing tricks on me. When the redheaded chick noticed me watching her she turned her head then walked away. I wanted to find Nino so I could bring the female to his attention. I didn't care if we just had an altercation. There was many questions that needed to be answered and plus she was going to get her ass kicked that night if nothing else. I walked through the crowd looking for him, but before I found him, I was approached by her. She extended her hand toward me and said, "I'm Sheena, Nino's baby momma." I looked at her like the fool she was. I wanted to reach out and touch her right then and there because she just confirmed what I needed to know so now all together she has disrespected on three different occasions.

"Excuse me, what did you say?" I said in between laughs while staring at her funny looking ass. It was bad enough she had fire red hair as dark as she was, but to top it off she had on a colorful outfit looking like a clown. All she needed was a red nose to complete her look.

"You heard me, I'm his baby momma," she said while putting her hand in my face.

"First of all you need to get your hand out of my face and secondly what the hell are you telling me for?" I replied while rolling my eyes and neck.

"You're the reason he don't take care of my shorty, and since you are the reason you need to be taking care of baby, Nino."

Who in the hell does she think she's talking to? This bitch has lost her rabbit ass mind. Whatever high tech drug she's taking, she needs to stay off it. I looked her up and down then stole on her directly in her face for disrespecting me for the fourth time. Sparkle and Buttah noticed Shenna and me fighting and ran over to where we were. They instantly jumped in the fight, with no questions asked. We took all of our anger and frustrations out on her. We kicked and punched her like she was a punching bag. Once again, security came and broke up the fight and asked what was going on. Before I could get a chance to explain, Sheena was charging toward me with a box cutter in her hand, but Buttah grabbed her by her hair yanking her back in place. I began explaining to the security guard how the confrontation started and about my previous run in with the chick. I asked Sparkle to find Nino so we could get to the bottom of this situation.

When Sparkle returned with Nino, he carried a look of hatred on his face and it was all directed toward Sheena.

Nino approached Sheena and asked, "What's the problem? Why you all up in my girl face?"

"Yo' girl? What you mean, 'yo' girl'? You told me I was yo' girl. You also said that you were going to do right by our son."

"Check this out. I'm not your son's father. The li'l bastard is light-skinned with grey eyes and curly hair. There's no way I can be his father. Look at me. I have nappy ass hair, dark brown eyes, and I'm darker than the soul of your shoe. How many times do I have to tell you that and I'm not your man, either. When was the last time I spoke with you?" There was a moment of silence. "Exactly, and when you call me do I pick up?" There was another moment of silence. "Exactly, so get the fuck on. It's over between me and you, and it has been for years."

I knew that he dated a girl name Sheena before we got together, but she never came across my path until now. I know he's still sleeping with the chic why else would she go out her way to damage my car and stalk me at the club. What she failed to realize is that she got the right bitch because I'm going to give her what she's looking for.

Nino and Sheena dated for about two years before he found out the type of chic she was. She was the type of hoe that stole his money, fucked, and sucked on his friends. With a man like Nino, why would you need to steal from him? He acts like money grows on trees. He definitely takes care of home first.

Nino had taken a business trip one weekend and returned home sooner than he planned. When he stuck his key in the door, he saw Sheena sucking on his friend like a lollipop, butt naked on their living room couch. He beat her ass and shot dude in both legs, so she knew that he was not to be played with.

"Fuck you, Nino; you ain't shit and you ain't ever gonna be sh…" Before she got a chance to finish her sentence, he slapped the bitch to the ground and I spit on the bitch for fucking with my car.

Holding the side of her face and getting off the floor, she screamed, "Watch your back, Nino. This isn't over."

"So you threatening me bitch? You know I don't

take threats lightly." The whole time the commotion was taking place the party was still going on as if an altercation was not happening. People were still dancing and getting their drink on, not paying us any attention, but we did have some onlookers. Nino looked as if he wanted to hit her again, so I took it upon myself and stole on her and we walked away.

I must admit, I do love Nino. I'd rather go to war with him than against him. Even though the love is there, I still realize our relationship has taken a turn for the worst. Lately he has been showing me a side of him that I thought I would never see. I'm tired of fighting with him over every little thing and then he tries to make it up by showering me with expensive gifts. I know after tonight I should be expecting a big gift. Nino grabbed me by my hand, looked me in my eyes, and gave me an apology for his actions and the incident with Sheena. I accepted his apologize only to keep the peace between me and him. Little did he know, I still planned to get away from him and this dysfunctional relationship.

About 20 minutes later, everyone was ducking from the loud gunshots ringing through the air. I didn't know exactly where they were coming from; I just went with my instincts and ducked. Three more shot went off, POW, POW, POW. Nino pulled me back down instantly. "Stay low baby, don't move, I'll be right back." Nino shouted sounding like the terminator. Shit rarely scares me, but without my gun I was terrified and tears were flowing down my face like a waterfall. I begged him not to leave me, but he did anyway. He instructed me to stay low and he promised me he'd be right back. As I glanced around everybody was screaming, crying, and praying to the man above. I've never been in a situation like this before. I hate being caught off guard. All I could do was curse myself for leaving my gun at home. I normally bring my gun out with me because anything is liable to happen in the club and this situation just proved my point.

All type of things was flashing through my mind because I haven't seen Buttah or Sparkle since Sheena came back shooting up the party. I hope they are all right. I wouldn't be able to live with myself if something happened to them on the account of me. I couldn't believe Sheena had gone crazy all on the account of a man. She was definitely trying to lay me or him if not both of us to rest. Then, all of a sudden, she caught me off guard and walked up behind me and said, "Die, bitch." I was in shock. I couldn't move at all. I was frozen in place. I knew my life was over at that point. I closed my eyes very tightly and said a silent prayer. I thought about all the good times I had growing up as a child. My mother provided me with an exceptional childhood until her boyfriend took her life. I also thought about how I would never get a chance to bare children or even become a bride. Even though I was leaving a lot behind, I was getting a second chance to be with my mother. My mind began to easy at the thought of being in her presence again. My thoughts were interrupted by a single gunshot.

Chapter Six
J-Boogie

"Get the fuck in the car now, Buttah and Sparkle," I spoke, with authority.

"Naw, J-Boogie. We can't leave Honeybun. We all came together so, therefore, we all were going to leave together."

"I understand that, but she's in there with her man and I'm quite sure he will take care of her. We need to leave before the police get here. I got heat in my car and I know you got heat in yours because you never leave home without it."

"You damn right I have heat in my car," Buttah stated with a jazzy attitude.

I watched as Buttah tossed Sparkle her keys to her car while instructing her to get the guns out of the trunk. Whatever Buttah says goes. Her friends weren't anything but her little foot soldiers. All I could do was shake my head and roll with my sister. After retrieving the guns, Sparkle tossed my sister a small-chromed 25 while she kept a black and silver one in her hand. One thing I can say is she a loyal motherfucker when it comes to the safety of her girls. Therefore, I ran to my car and grabbed my pistol and we headed in the opposite direction the crowd was running in. With gun in hand, we went back inside the club in search of Honeybun. We searched the crowd as they ran pass, but she was nowhere to be found.

I yelled to Buttah, "Let's get the fuck out of here; I don't see your girl or her guy nowhere in sight and plus I'm sure the police is near."

"One more minute, J, I know she's in here somewhere. Look over there by VIP."

I headed toward VIP and there still was no Honeybun. "Are you happy now? I'm sure her and her guy got out safe. He's a gangsta, right? He knows how to handle himself."

Instantly, I grabbed Buttah and Sparkle's guns from their hands because the police were now entering the club. One of my buddies was a bouncer at the club, so I got his attention and I passed him the guns along with $500 just to hold them so we could get out safely.

Seconds later, a police yelled in our direction and told us to get the fuck out of the club. With no hesitation, I yelled, "No problem, officer, we don't want any trouble."

A short, fat detective got the uniform cop attention that was talking to us and our eyes followed. We noticed they were surrounding a body that was on the floor in front of the men's bathroom, but we all knew it was a lady because she was lying there with one stiletto on and the other one was lying adjacent to her feet. Instantly, all three of us took off in that direction. The officers drew their guns and began yelling and telling us to get the fuck back or they were going to arrest us.

"Didn't I just tell you three a minute ago to get the fuck out of here? Do you motherfuckas wanna go to jail?"

"No need for that, Mr. Officer. All we wanted to see if that's our friend lying on the floor or not because we can't find her." Not saying another word to us, the officers began to hold a conversation amongst each other as if they were ignoring what I just said out my mouth.

"Aye, you come here," a tall, skinny officer with red hair pointed and shouted at Sparkle. Sparkle walked over to where they were in her four-inch pumps. The officers were in awe as she walked toward them. Their mouth hung wide open as the black beauty approached them. They just didn't know that I had the best view in the house. With every step she took, her ass bounced from side to side taking me down memory lane. I thought about all the things she used to do to me that had me giving her all my money with no problem. I snapped out of my daze as she finally approached the body as one of the officers removed a red tablecloth that covered the girl's face. To our relief, Sparkle yelled out, "It's not her, it's Sheena.

$$$$$$$$

Back at my condo, Buttah and I discussed what our next move was going to be. There were plenty of niggas in the street getting money so that meant there was plenty of money for us to take. I never believed in working hard to get what I wanted. I believe in taking what I wanted. My crew and I were taking the streets by storm one day at a time. We had these simple ass niggas watching over their shoulders because they didn't know which way we were coming. We tried to keep a low profile so majority of our jobs were done out of town, but if we saw a nigga slipping in our city he was definitely a target. I knew what I had my sister doing was beyond dangerous, but her love for them dead presidents wouldn't let her stay away from my hustle.

Every weekend my sister and I go club hopping with one thing on our agenda "money." Even though Honeybun and Sparkle tagged along, they weren't apart of the team. Unbeknownst to Sparkle, she hadn't the slightest clue as to what we were doing, but Honeybun knew exactly what was going on. She used to be part of the team until she met Nino. After they became an item, she did a 180 and decided she didn't want to hustle with us anymore, which was fine by me.

Upon going to the clubs, we made sure that we always arrived and left at different times because we didn't want anyone to know that we were together. Many didn't know that Buttah and I were sisters and brothers. Even though we are not blood sister and brother, I still have a lot of love for her. My father married her mother and the moment they became one, we became one.

I really hate this weekend things didn't go as planned and went down the way that it did because there were a lot of drunk niggas that could have got hit that night especially that dude Dough Boy. I haven't seen him in the clubs in a while and tonight would have been a great opportunity to follow him back to his house. He is one hustler that I'm determined to get. I knew fucking with him was risky, but if I hit him where it hurt, I will not have to rob another low life nigga for the rest of my life.

Ever since me and my crew wacked his right hand man, Dough Boy has been trying to keep a low profile so seeing him at the club was a total surprise. All his right hand man Lil Joe had to do, was open the safe with the drugs and the money, but no, he wanted to act like a tax paying citizen and try to resolve the situation.

Setting Lil Joe up took a lot of planning to do, but eventually with my hard work of stalking him it all paid off and everybody went home happy. I was like a private investigator on his ass. I was taking photos of his every move and peeking through windows until I found out where his safe was. Once I found out where the safe was that's when I put Buttah on his ass. She was my entry into the house. I normally don't go on the actual job, that's the purpose of me having a crew, but I knew from the beginning Lil Joe was going to be a problem so I tagged along.

"Nigga, open the motherfuckin' safe," I said, as I pointed a Desert Eagle at Li'l Joe's head while he was tied to a chair.

"Bitch ass nigga, I'm not opening shit. Kiss my ass," he shouted.

I couldn't believe he was talking shit with this big a gun pointed at his head. I guess he thought I came from a bloodline full of bitch ass niggas, but he had me messed up. I hit him with the butt of the gun and blood instantly ran from his forehead down his face. I asked him several more times to open the safe, but he kept talking shit. All I wanted was the money and the drugs, but he was pushing my buttons and I knew before I left his house he was going to be a corpse. I guess he had too much pride to bitch up since there was a sexy lady in the room, but what he didn't know was the sexy lady worked for me.

Buttah even tried pleading with him. I guess she saw murder in my eyes and she wanted to spare his life. Murder is something that I try to stay away from, but like 2Pac said, *I'm not a killer, but don't push me.*

"Lil Joe can you please just give him the money so we can all walk out of here alive. Money comes and goes. I have a child to look after," Buttah stated, while pleading with dude.

I almost laughed when I heard her mention a child, knowing damn well she doesn't have any kids. He wasn't trying to hear that shit though. He even became disrespectful toward her. He began shouting that she probably set the whole thing up. Even though he was speaking the truth, what fucked him up is when he called Buttah out her name. Buttah hated a disrespectful ass nigga. Since he was searching for the truth, she gave him the truth. She snatched that big ass gun out my hand and pointed it in his face. Lil Joe's eyes grew as big as a cantaloupe.

"Now I'm running this show, motherfucka," Buttah shouted, with nothing but pure anger in her voice. "You can make this hard or you can make this simple as one, two, three. It's your choice. Now open up the safe and give us the fucking drugs and money or I'm gonna rock your ass to sleep for eternity."

"I'm not givin' you sh…" Buttah put him to sleep with his brain splattered on the wall.

Buttah what the hell you do that for. I wanted to smoke the fool," I stated, laughing.

Buttah didn't say a word she just looked at me with a smirk on her face while tossing me back my gun. She proceeded, took her gun out of her small handbag, went straight for the safe, and shot it open. We really were trying to avoid using our guns, but some things are not avoidable. Instantly, I phoned Gunz, one of my loyal workers, and told him to come in with the duffel bags. The whole time we were inside, he sat outside in a stolen car making sure we didn't have any unexpected visitors.

I went over to Lil Joe's dead body and took every piece of jewelry he had on, spit on him, and called him a stupid motherfucka. He would be still alive if he had cooperated. Once we clean out the safe, I set fire to the house and we made a run for it.

Chapter Seven
SPARKLE

*I*t's a typical day in the ghetto as I head to the gym. Driving down Chicago Avenue the sun was beaming making my new paint job on my car glisten. I stared out my tinted windows relaxing under AC, while looking at the neighborhood hustlers go about their everyday routine, which consisted of standing on the corner, shooting dice, smoking weed, or slinging drugs. All I could do was shake my head at the petty hustlers. Pulling up and stopping at a red light I glanced at my gas hand on my car and realized I was running low on fuel. Not wanting to stop for gas, I pulled over, turned the AC off, and dropped the top on my BMW so I could make it to and from the gym without any problems.

Finally pulling up at the gym, I jumped out my

vehicle, threw my Puma duffle bag on my shoulder, and headed inside. Once inside, I spotted Buttah and Honeybun on the treadmill getting there workout on. I headed straight for the locker room, got dressed in my puma work out gear, and joined my buddies.

"What's up chicks?" I said before I got on the treadmill next to Honeybun. They both waved at me. They didn't speak a word because they were out of breath. We continued our work out for the next hour and a half incorporating more cardio on the stair master and weight lifting, and then we hit the showers to freshen up.

"What a work out?" Buttah stated as she threw her hair in a ponytail.

"I really needed that," stated Honeybun as she tied her shoes.

"Yes we all needed that to clear our minds." I stated while zipping my duffle bag.

Exiting the gym, we all headed straight toward Buttah's Range Rover to discuss the incident that took place at the club for the very first time. I couldn't believe Nino killed that girl, but I'm glad that he did because if he didn't believe me Honeybun was going to hunt that bitch down like an animal and skin her alive. Don't let the pretty faces and big asses fool you, me and my girls gets down for ours. All I can say is Nino must have the bomb between his legs to make a chick go crazy like that. I know me and Nino never gotten along, but I have mad respect for that dude now. He definitely handled his business that night. One thing I can say is even though he disrespects Honeybun, he's wasn't going to let Sheena get away with disrespecting her. In a way, I felt sorry for the girl. I also felt sorry for her child who will grow up with no parents. The mother was dead and the father was who knows who. The way she loved him, I pray I will never experience love like that. Love can make people do some crazy things. R.I.P. Sheena.

"So, Honeybun," I spoke clearing my throat. "How do you feel about what happened at the club?"

"Girl, it's whateva. The bitch had it coming. She knew what type of guy Nino was, so why would she put herself in a position like that? Even if he didn't handle his business, I definitely was gonna handle mine and if you're asking do I feel sorry for her, the answer to your question is hell no."

"Do you even care about her child not having any parents?"

"No I don't care. That's not my problem. Once again, she put herself in that position. If Nino was messing with Sheena, all she had to do was play her role of being the sideline hoe. Don't tell me you starting to go soft on us." Honeybun replied.

"It's not about going soft. It was just a question." I snapped back with an attitude.

"We ride or die chicks," Buttah intervened. "No matter what happened that night we can't change anything. We just have to move forward like nothing ever happened so as of today let's not bring Sheena name up again.

Even though we all agreed not to bring Sheena name up I couldn't stop thinking about that incident. Maybe I was turning soft, but only because there was a child involved. I believed every child deserved to be raised by loving parents and Nino took that away from that child. I really have been considering giving up this crazy lifestyle and trading it for a normal one. The shooting at the club was just too close to home for me and it was definitely an eye opener. That could have been anyone of us lying on the floor dead.

Lately I find myself wondering why I wasn't born into a stable environment where I didn't have to struggle and turn tricks just to get by. I want to live life without thinking about where my next meal is going to come from and if the person I just slept with is going to give me a disease. Right before sex, I say a prayer, strange right, and question the person about their sex life and hope they are being honest with me. I do that because I don't use condoms, they break me out into a bad rash so I just pray that whomever I'm sleeping with don't give me a deadly disease. In due time I will change or will I. Is it possible to change when you've been so accustom to a certain lifestyle?

$$\$\$\$\$\$\$\$\$$$

After the workout and brief conversation, I headed straight home to get some much-needed rest. I lay in bed for a while before I actually dozed off. Jumping up out of my sleep, I looked at my clock only to realize I've been sleep for 15minutes. Damn I cursed myself and threw my plush pillow over my head. This actually has been going on for the past few nights since I haven't spoken with Bone. Each time I wake out of my sleep, all that clouds my mind is the way Buttah was looking at him the night we were headed to the club. Even though she is my buddy, there are a lot of things that she does that I don't agree with. First and foremost she's a backstabber, but only when money and men are involved. She would sleep with anybody if the price was right. She even stooped as low as to sleep with her own stepfather. When I heard that, I couldn't believe my ears. How can any woman sleep behind their own mother? That's simply disgusting. I really do believe that we are going to fall out over some street nigga. She has no boundaries when it comes to money. She would do anything to get that mighty dollar. I don't know why she didn't think I would find out that she tricked off with Lil Thug, Kevin, and Smoke. What she failed to realize is that men gossip more than females do. I never brought it to her attention because I'm not a petty female when it comes to men. I change men like I change my underwear. So just as fast as each one of them left, another trick came along. If any bitch can fuck what's supposed to be mine, he was never mine to begin with. I'm not mad that she had sex with them, I'm mad at the fact that she didn't ask me to join knowing that we make an awesome tag team. One thing that she has to know is that payback is a bitch. When the time is right, I will definitely strike back because she messed me over not one time, not two times, but three times. I know times get hard, but that still don't give her the right to trick off with my male friends behind my back.

Waking up the next morning, I felt restless. I still didn't get the proper rest that I needed. Between tossing and turning all night and thinking about Bone, I was a total wreck. I didn't want to get out of bed for nothing in the world. I glanced at my cell phone and house phone in hopes that I had at least one missed call from him. However, when I glanced at the phones, my hopes were broken. The wheels in my head started to turn because Bone never goes a day without calling me and it has been at least 3 days now. I just didn't understand why he hasn't called. We didn't have any type of confrontation so I do not understand why he's being so distance. I just hope nothing has happened to him.

Even though I dread getting out the bed I had to because I needed to get ready for the weekend and I needed to do some shopping. I picked up my cell phone, glanced through my contacts to see whose man I can hit up. Even though I had my on cash, nothing felt better than spending some else's money. Everybody that I called either was busy, or wasn't picking up. Even Bone, out of all people, still wasn't picking up his phone, something was definitely wrong and I was determined to find out. I called Bone's phone three times back to back and still didn't get an answer. Calling him or any man like that was out of character for me, but my woman's intuition kicked in, that's why I kept calling. My intuition was telling me that he was with another woman. I really couldn't get mad because we never officially said we were a couple. We were just doing us and we did us quite often. I hate being ignored so I continued to call several more time and still he didn't answer. Sooner or later, he will be calling me and I will just play the same games he just played with me. I knew for a fact that he was with a female. I should go to his crib, but I went with my better judgment and stayed put.

Despite Bone answering his phone he is a cool nigga. He's someone I have considered settling down with once I finish living my life of a young beautiful diva. Being in a committed relationship is something that I just can't handle right now, but when the time is right, he will be the first person to be considered. I'm going to call him one more time. If he picks up, he picks up and if he doesn't, oh well, his loss not mines. I dialed his seven digits one last time and on the second ring, he decided to pick up.

"Hello," he said, sounding out of breath. I could hear the sweet melody of R. Kelly's *12 play,* serenading the air.

"Are you busy?" I asked with an attitude. At this point, I was beyond pissed. First of all I haven't spoken with his ass in a couple of days which lead me to believe that something probably happened to him, secondly he's playing phone game, and lastly to put the icing on the cake when he answered the phone he was breathing like he had just ran a 20 mile marathon.

"Yea, I'm busy," he said, then hung up the phone. I couldn't believe he did that, but guess what I'm not in the business to be sweating any man, so I'm going to let him be.

Chapter Eight
BUTTAH

"Oooh! Ah! Yes, baby! This pussy is the bomb. Whose is it?" Chris said, as he humped in and out of my douched, tight pussy.

"It's yours baby, keep giving it to me," I said not feeling a damn thing. This nigga really thinks he's putting it on me.

He humped on me for about three minutes before he yelled out, "I'm cummin'."

"Cum on, baby, mama cummin' with you."

I could have won an Oscar for the performance I was putting on. I wanted to smack the shit out of him for bragging on his manhood that turned out to be his childhood. I hate when brother's brag on their genitals just to get a female in bed. If it weren't for the money, he never would have gotten the time of day. I grabbed my drink that was sitting on the table across from the queen size bed that we were lying in and downed it with one gulp. After what I just went through I needed that, I spoke quietly to myself.

Chris jumped into the shower to wash away the scent of bootie, pussy, and dick, so his wife wouldn't smell it once he made it home.

I quickly grabbed my cell phone from my Gucci purse to see if I had any missed calls, voicemails, or text messages. I had several missed calls and voicemails and five were from Sparkle. Every message she left said the same thing, "Girl, where you at? You've been M.I.A. for a couple of days. Call me when you get this message." I made a mental note to myself to call her first chance I get. The other missed calls and voicemails that I received were from my male friends.

When I heard the shower stop, I immediately tossed my phone back into my purse. The bathroom door open slowly then seconds later Chris walked out the bathroom with a towel wrap around the lower part of his body. With water still dripping from his face and upper body, I instantly was turned on like a light switch. Even though his penis was little and he couldn't fuck me past three minutes, for some strange reason, I was still attracted to him without a doubt. God deserve an award for making him that fine.

I met him at the doorway of the bathroom and grabbed the towel he had wrapped around his waist. I dried his upper body off then licked his chest. I slowly made my way down on my knees. I sucked his balls while I massaged his penis. He ran his fingers through my hair to let me know that he was enjoying every moment I had him in my mouth. In a matter of seconds, he was putting his babies down my throat, and then we fell asleep in the comfort of each other arms. About thirty minutes into my beauty rest I was awakened my several loud knocks at the door. I tried to ignore the knocks, but the knocks just wouldn't stop. I turned toward Chris to wake him, but he wouldn't bulge. I guess I really put it on him.

"Chris, Chris, somebody is knocking on the door." I spoke while trying to shake him awake again. He just laid there in a deep sleep not hearing a word I was saying. I shook him several more times, "Chris, get up I think your wife is at the door." He jumped up as fast as he could after I made that statement.

"What you say?" he responded while rubbing his eyes and sitting up in the bed.

"You heard me. Get up somebody is at the door," I retorted while pointing in the direction the knocks were coming from.

"It's probably no one, but room service." He jumped out the bed threw on a robe and headed toward the door.

"Who is it?" Chris yelled out.

"Housekeeping," a high-pitched male voice answered from the other side of the door. "Sir, I'm sorry to bother you, but I just wanted to drop off some clean towels before my shift ended."

Chris hesitated for a brief moment then looked at me and mouthed the words "I can't believe you woke me up for the shit."

"I'm sorry baby. Don't be made at me." I said trying to sound like a child that was trying to con her mom out of something. "The sooner you open the door, the sooner he can leave, and the sooner I can put you back to sleep." I spoke while winking my eye at him and rubbing on my twins that were a perfect size double "D" thanks to Dr. Grochowshik. When Chris caught my drift, he couldn't do anything, but smile.

Chris grabbed the towels from housekeeping, threw them on the couch, and headed back to bed with me. I heard the vibrations of my phone coming from my purse. Flashing across the screen of my phone, I noticed the words 'a family and two kids.' All I could do was shake my head and I text back 'no a family, four kids, and a dog' which meant I was in room 241.

"Hey, what your sexy ass doing baby," he asked me because my upper body was leaning out the bed.

"Nothing much baby. I'm just texting my girl back. She was worried about me 'cause I haven't been answering my phone and I just wanted to let her know that everything was all right."

"Oh, okay."

"All finish. Now I can give you my undivided attention without any more interruptions from my cell phone."

He reached over, grabbed me, and placed me in

a straddling position on his lap and as soon as we begin kissing there were more knocks at the door.

"Fuck" he shouted out and threw me gently off his lap.

As soon as Chris unlocked the door, it flew wide open knocking him on the floor.

"What the fuck?" I yelled out playing my role while grabbing the thick white comforter to cover up my body as three men barged into the room with masks on their face asking for money.

"We don't have any money." I cried out.

"Bitch you might not, but your boyfriend does." The tallest guy out the crew walked over to me, snatched the cover off my body, and admired my tall tower. I then grabbed a pillow from the bed to cover my private area, but he snatched that away too. He then raised his left hand, which met my face, and I began to scream from the pain my face just encountered.

The heaviest of the three, grabbed Chris by his throat, tossed him on the bed, and demanded a hundred thousand dollars from him. The guy told him he had one hour to have someone drop the money off to a secluded location. For the first couple of minutes Chris was denying being capable of putting his hands on that amount of money, but with a few blows to the head and ribs, he gave in like the bitch he is.

Chris proceeded to call his wife. As he pressed each button on the phone, a tear fell from his eyes. I couldn't believe he was crying like a little girl who had just lost her favorite toy. I wanted to tell him to man up. He informed his wife Tori not to ask any question and to do what he asks because his life depended on it. He also informed her not to contact the authorities. I could hear her on the other end of the phone from where I was standing hollering and screaming. I felt kind of sorry for her because she wasn't sure if her husband was going to live or not, even if she gave up the money.

I've only known Chris for two days before he let me in his bedroom. Being blessed with a pretty face, phat ass, and a cute smile can get you into any man's bed. I met him one weekend when I was flying out of town to handle some business for my brother. I sat across from him on the plane. Our eyes connected a couple of times before him and his friend began to speak so freely about how much money they have and all the businesses they own from state to state. A real bitch recognizes game, and I was willing to call his bluff. I listened attentively while they continue to brag to each other about who stocks were doing better and who wife has the biggest ring. What really grabbed my attention was when Chris started talking about the fleet of cars he has parked at his mansion that wasn't too far from the Miami International Airport.

Once off the plane, he asked to carry my Louis Vuitton duffle bag. I told him "yes" without any hesitation. His six foot two solid body looked good as hell and so did his friend's. I imagined having sex with both of them. If the price was right, who knows what could have gone down behind closed doors. We talked for a couple of minutes, asking each other the basic questions like what's your name, where you from, and how old are you? After our brief conversation, Chris walked me to my limo that awaited me. We exchanged numbers and agreed to have dinner before I left town. Little did he know, this would be the night he regretted meeting me. It's a shame how weak-minded a man is when it comes to the P.U.S.S.Y.

$$$$$$$$$

Once back from Miami, I sat on my bed and unpacked my Louis Vuitton duffle bag, and counted out my part of the money I earned from the robberies. I told my brother not to let the dude who smack me on any more jobs. He smacked me just a little bit too hard and I hated the way he stared at me with his evil looking eyes. I walked away with $45,000 for robbing Chris, my brother $25,000 and the other three guys $10,000 apiece. I walked away with the most because I was the put my brother up on that particular hustle. The only thing he had to do was send the men, and follow my lead. I knew Chris was going to be an easy target because he was to open about what he had and he wanted me to see how he was living.

Initially I went to Miami to set this nigga up that my brother had been watching. My first night in Miami we robbed him. He was another easy target. I thought it was going to be hard since J-Boogie told me he had been watching him for quite some time. Actually, he was the easiest nigga I ever set up. I didn't even have to spread my legs open for him. Blue was the name he went by.

As soon as I stepped into my hotel room to settle in, I received a call from my brother letting me know Blue's whereabouts. I freshened up a little and headed straight to the club on Washington and 17th where he was so I could work my number. When I spotted him in the club, my first thought was, *he's a lot darker than his picture.* Even though he was darker, I knew I had the right person because everything else about him was the same. I headed straight over to where he was and started shaking my ass in front of him to an old school mix. I could tell he was memorized by my body. I shook my ass like I was a professional stripper. I even made sure I did my specialty dance and made my ass clap. After getting him to the point of no return, I whispered sweet and sexual things in his ear. Twenty minutes later, we were pulling up to his gorgeous home. Upon entry to his house, I was amazed by his exquisite and unique taste in furniture. He definitely wasn't your average hood nigga. We sat on the couch having small talk, drinking Nuvo and Hennessey. I could tell he wasn't a drinker because the first half of cup he had, he was tipsy and at the club, the only drink he had was a bottle of water. I asked him to get up to get me some ice so I could put a chill to my drink. As he proceeded toward the kitchen, I slipped him a couple of drops of Visine in his drink. When he returned with my ice, we continued to talk until his drink was all gone. Shortly after that, he was knocked out on the couch looking lifeless. I quickly took out my phone and texted one of my brother's workers the address to where I was. While waiting for the others to arrive, I went in the kitchen and fixed me something to eat. Going through his subzero refrigerator I noticed he had left over's from Popeye's so I warmed that up then head back in the living room, propped my feet up on his cocktail table and watched a movie on his 70inch flat screen.

When the two guys arrived, they went from room to room searching for the money. J Boogie knew the money was there in the house somewhere, but didn't know exactly where. All he knew was he would see Blue go in the house with duffels bags every day at the same time and when he left the house he was empty handed. He knew it was money or drug. It really didn't matter what it was as long as we came out with a profit. We preferred money though because we really weren't into the drug game. Having straight cash just made the payout much easier. One of the guys headed upstairs while the other guy searched the basement of the house. In the process of me waiting, all I heard was glass being broken, drawers being pulled out, and mattresses being flipped over. A couple of minutes later, I heard the guy from upstairs scream, "Bingo." When I heard the magic word, I knew that he had hit the jackpot. I yelled to the basement for the other guy and then I headed upstairs. I had to keep a close eye on these niggas because I trust no one especially when money is involved. Dude had come across twelve bricks and several bags of money, which was tucked away in the back of a walk in closet. Some niggas are so damn typical. Why would anyone keep all their money and dope where they lay their head? Honestly, I can understand keeping your money in arms reach, but drugs that a stupid move on anyone's behalf. All that matters is that I got that job done, and my pockets are fatter than what they were before.

After reminiscing about what I've done over the weekend, several minutes later I received a call from the front desk letting me know there was a gentleman down there to see me. I didn't ask any questions. I just told the desk clerk to send him right up because I automatically thought it was J-Boogie. *I hope he don't have another job lined up already for me; shit I just got back in town.* J-Boogie knows I hate unexpected guest so I'm assuming him showing up unexpectedly had to be very important. I reached toward my dresser to retrieve my cell phone to make sure I didn't miss any calls from him and I hadn't. I quickly threw my money back in my duffel bag and tossed it underneath my bed.

Knock Knock Knock

"Come in; it's open," I shouted.

Knock Knock Knock

"Come in; the door is open," I shouted again, but a little louder so he could hear me from the bedroom.

Knock Knock Knock

Damn, I know he hear me. Any other time he comes barging through the door with his key, "Here I come," I screamed.

Walking through my crib, I was pissed off and was prepared to curse J out for two reasons, one for showing up at my place unexpectedly and two for knocking on my door like he has lost his fucking mind.

When I swung the door open, I couldn't believe no one was there. *What the fuck?* I was beyond pissed because somebody was at my damn door playing games. As soon as I closed my door and got halfway back to my bedroom, the knocking started again. I yelled out, "Who is it?" Of course, there was no response and that pissed me off even more. I continue and headed to my bedroom and called J to see if he would answer his phone and he didn't so I assumed again that it was him playing at the door, but what's with the games. Immediately after I hung up the phone the knocks started back. I smiled and headed back toward the door with my phone in hand, but before reaching the door, it was J calling me back.

"J, why in the hell you at my door playing?"

"What are you talking about, sis? I'm way across town that's not me at your door." Instantly my antennas went up. *Who could this be, playing at my door?*

There was a moment of silence between us before J responded. "Are you all right, Buttah? What's wrong? I'm on my way over."

"Nothing is wrong, J. I'm good there's no need to come over. I'm pretty sure it's the kids in the building playing at my door again," I lied "Don't worry about me, finish doing what you were doing."

"All right, Buttah, call me later; I need to talk to you about something anyway so make sure you call me. Love ya."

"Love you, too." I hung up the phone, headed straight to my bedroom, and grabbed my gun. Motherfuckas trying to play with my head. Their asses are going to feel some heat if they don't stop playing with me. The knocks started again. I called the front desk and asked the front desk clerk what was the person's name that sign in.

With shame in his voice he stated, "Sorry, but the guy didn't sign in. Since you told me to send him right up, I assumed you knew exactly who he was. Is everything all right? Do you need me to call the police?"

"There no need to call the police, I was just asking because he hasn't made it upstairs to the apartment yet."

"Oh okay, well call me if you need anything."

I hung the phone up immediately. I couldn't get mad because I did tell him to send the guy straight up, but if he were doing his job correctly, he would have still made him sign in no matter what.

Marching toward the door, with gun in hand, I swung the door open and peeked out and of course, there was nobody there. Instead of me going back into the crib, I walked down the hall checking stairs cases, any other place a person could hide, and of course, I didn't see anybody hiding anywhere. Putting my gun on safety and on my hip, I walked back to my apartment.

Slamming the door behind me, I instantly felt a cold barrel pressed against the temple of my head. I couldn't believe I was caught slipping. When I turned to face the gunman, I was face to face with a clown mask.

The gunman backed hand me and I went flying to the ground. I rose slowly holding the side of my face with my mouth hung wide open. I couldn't muster up a word. I was in total shock. He began to pat me down and he retrieved the gun that I was carrying in my waistline. The expression on my face said it all. "Bitch, get up. You're not so tough without your gun are you?" He continued to slap and punched me before he asked where the money was.

"I have no money what are you talking about."

"Bitch, so you want to play with me right," he shouted with so much anger in his voice.

Once again, he smacked me and I fell to the floor, but this time he kicked me one good time in my stomach. I cradled my stomach as if I was cradling a newborn child. I was in so much pain, but I refused to shed a tear.

I looked up at him and stated, "When I get my hands on..." He choked me, cutting me off in mid-sentence.

"When you get your hands on me what? What you gonna do? You one tough bitch I see?" After each word, he continued punching me like a punching bag. "Now give me the money so I can go."

All I was thinking about was the hard work I put in for the money. Now I have to give it up. I guess what goes around comes around. He yelled out again, "Bitch where is the money, I'm not going to continue to play with you."

Dude start beating the shit out of me, from slaps, to punches, to kick I felt defeated. I never felt defeated before. The only reason why I was taking the ass whopping is because he had the upper hand by having a gun. If there weren't any gun involved, it wouldn't have been this easy. No matter the gender of a person or what size I'm going to put up a fight. Dude picked me up by my neck, dragged me to my bedroom, and threw me on the bed. He began to take off his shirt, then his pants. Standing there with nothing, but boxers on, my mind got to wondering. *What the fuck is he doing? Is this nigga about to rape me? Oh hell no, I'm not going.*

"Once I get through treating you like the hoe you are, I want the money and if you hesitate, I'm gonna kill you." He continued undressing himself then he snatched my shirt off and engulfed my right breast in his mouth while his other hand explored the lower part of my body. Making me lift the bottom part of my body off the bed, he snatched my pants off. He's moaned in pleasure while fingering me and still sucking on my breast. I tried pushing him off me, but he was just too strong. Forcing my legs apart, he inserted his manhood inside of me. I still didn't know the identity to the man behind the mask. As he continued to hump in and out of me, I continued to try to fight him off me, but there was no use. I finally gave up the fight and just laid there like a dead corpse. He continued to take advantage of my body and made his way downtown. As his tongue made love to my clitoris, tears began to flow down my face. "You like that baby," he asked. I didn't reply at all. "I love you, Buttah." I couldn't believe what I was hearing. Dude definitely has a loose screw somewhere. Dude was robbing me, yet he was infatuated with me. The moment he felt like he had total control, I reached under my pillow, pulled out my other gun, and shot him one time in the head. His brain fragments were all over my body. I jumped up and immediately took his mask off his face. I couldn't believe the face that was staring back at me. It was one of J-boogie's workers. The same people smacked the shit out of me in Miami when we were robbing Chris. All I could do was shake my head at his money hungry ass. Dude made a nice penny working for my brother, but I guess one can never have too much money. I'm glad I had the silencer on the gun because I stood over his body and shot his body up leaving one bullet in the chamber. I politely point the gun at his dick and shot that motherfucker off. Dude had violated me and I hope his sorry ass burn in hell. I immediately called J-boogie and he came right off and helped me dispose the body with no problem.

Chapter Nine
HONEYBUN

*W*ith a frustrated look spread across my face I entered my home and stared at the trail of white and red rose pedals from the doorway to the top of the stairs. All I could do was shake my head at Nino's pathetic attempt to reconcile the situation. Walking into my living room, I noticed that it looked like a funeral home with all the arrangement of flowers that Nino had purchased for me. There was a card placed on the table that read, *Please accept my apology for the things that I've put you through. I want things back the way they used to be. I hope you can find it in your heart to forgive me. You're my queen. You're my everything, Love Nino.*

Tears immediately filled my eyes, but they weren't tears of joy. "Fuck you, Nino," I stated, out loud as if he was there. "You can't keep doing this to me."

Nino has caused me so much pain and I hope he didn't think that some lousy flowers were going to make things better. His apologetic role wasn't going to work this time. I've pleaded with him time and time again to get his shit together, but my crying and begging just didn't work. My heart can't endure any more pain.

I headed upstairs to my bedroom and shook my head at the sight of a black, silk gown from La Perla lying across my bed, with a small gift box sitting on top of it. Opening the gift box, I admired a pair of platinum pear shaped 4kt diamond earrings. More tears filled my eyes. I threw the gift box on the dresser knocking a picture of me and Nino on the floor and breaking it. Nino thinks just because he showers me with expensive gifts I'm supposed to forget about all the things he takes me through.

I know I said I was going to leave him, but after that horrific incident with Sheena, I didn't have enough courage to do it. I was too scared of what he might do to me if I left. I've really been trying to convince myself that he do love me, if he'll kill for me or was that really the case. Did love really have anything to do with him killing Sheena or was he just trying to save his own life.

Honestly, I thought our relationship was going to get a lot better after that, but of course, it didn't get better at all. Actually, it got worse. I began to receive anonymous calls to my cell phone. At first, the calls started out as me just hearing the other person's breathing on the other end. Then the calls graduated to threats. On a day-to-day basis, I would receive threats from females telling me if I didn't leave Nino alone they were going to finish what Sheena didn't. I'm not sure if the threats were coming from different females or not, all I knew was I was receiving these calls all day non-stop and on the nights he didn't come home, that's when I would receive calls hearing him fucking the shit out of some hood rat. Blaming Nino for the sexual acts wasn't an educational guess. I knew it was him because the female made sure when she set the calls up, it came directly from his cell phone. Hubby would flash across the screen of my phone and it didn't make it any better that she was screaming his name in the background.

When I told Nino about the calls I've been receiving of course he denied cheating. I even pressed the record button on my phone to record the sexual acts. When I played the recording back for him to hear, he still denied it was him and that somebody was just playing a joke to get under my skin, but I knew better. After letting him hear the recording the other day, all of a sudden I walk in the house and stumble across the rose pedals, the gown, and the earrings. I know Nino is a wanted man by the ladies, but there is a way of doing things. No female is supposed to be able to get close to me, know my number, know what I look like, or even know where we live. These bitches not even supposed to breathe the same air that I breathe. At all time he's supposed to have his sideline hoes under control.

Believe me when I tell you I'm not in denial

about our relationship. I know he's an asshole and I deserve better, but for the last four years, I've invested my time in him and groomed him into the man I wanted him to be. He's not going to get away with hurting me that easily. I'm going to stick around and play his game and at the same time, I'm going to take him for every penny he got. When I'm finished with him, he's going to hate that he even knows me.

First, I'm going to start with our joint bank accounts then his personal accounts. I have access to everything. I have all account numbers, pin numbers, his birth certificate, and his social security number. Hell, I even got his mother and father social security number and if they want to get on bullshit with me, I'll burn their asses, too. I'm going to start taking money out the accounts day by day and before he can blink his eyes, all the money will be gone. Secondly, I'm going to put the house up for sale. The house is in my name so I don't need his approval for anything. Next, I'm going to sale the cars that he keeps in storage and of course, all of those are in my name, too. I even know where the trap house is at. Shit I'm definitely going to make sure the police find out about that. He gave me too much access to his life and now he's trying to fuck me, that where he messed up at. Naw, nigga, it's fuck you. I just hope he has a backup plan. His better hope when I send him to jail one of his bitches has enough money to bond him out or enough money to get him a lawyer. What he failed to realize is that I'm the HBIC (Head Bitch in

Charge).

After giving me and Nino's relationship another long thought, I walked into the master bathroom and flushed the earrings down the toilet and went down stair to start the fireplace and threw the gown in it along with the card. With the money I'm about to come into I can afford to buy plenty more.

$$\mathscr{SSSSSSSS}$$

It was a quarter to seven a.m. when I heard Nino putting his key in the door. I was sleep in the living room on our custom made couch that he paid an arm and leg for because I was tired of sleeping in our big as bed alone. I didn't realize what time it was until I glanced at the custom-made Swarovski Crystal clock that hung over the fireplace and that infuriated me. He thinks just because he pays all the bills he can do what he wants. I got a trick for his ass. Tomorrow he will be walking into an empty house. I'm going to show him how it feels to sleep alone.

When I sat up on the couch, he glanced at me, not saying a word then proceeded to walk up our spiral stairs and headed straight to the bathroom. When I heard the bathroom door slam shut, I immediately ran up the stairs and knocked on the locked door. As I stood knocking, I heard the sink water running and I yelled out his name, but he didn't answer. Each time my fist hit the wood door the angrier I became. Nino just doesn't care about my feelings at all anymore. I definitely have to put my plan in affect right away. It's time he gets a taste of his own medicine. I continued to bang on the door, and he still wouldn't answer. When the water stopped, the door opened. He walked straight pass me smelling like zest soap not saying a word and headed straight to our bedroom. This nigga was really tripping.

"Nino, what's yo' motherfuckin' problem?" I yelled, while approaching him with my two-piece lingerie on looking sexy as hell. You would have thought by me standing there in my two pieces, I would've caught his attention, but I didn't. I wanted him to grab me and make love to me despite what we've going through and him just walking in the house. I wanted him to make me feel like I felt when we first met.

"Ain't nothing wrong with me, I'm just tired and a little aggravated, that all." Who in the hell do he think he's talking to. First, he walked in the house totally ignoring me as if I wasn't there, secondly he runs straight to the bathroom and washed off his dick, and lastly the only excuse he can give me for his actions is that he's tired and aggravated...what the fuck?

"If you would have brought you ass in the house a couple of hours earlier, you wouldn't be so tired. I don't know who or what have you in the streets all night long, but something has to give. I'm tired of sleeping in our house by myself. If I wanted to live by myself I would have told you so, and on top of that, we don't even make love to me anymore."

"Is that what this all about, sex? Sex doesn't pay the bills Heidi, me busting my ass in the streets twenty-four hours a day is what pays the bills. It's too early in the morning for this shit. Now take your ass back downstairs with that bullshit before I slap the fuck out of you."

The only time he calls me by my government name is when he's guilty of something. "Nigga, you ain't gonna do shit to me, but I'll do me and you a favor. Instead of me going downstairs, I'm gonna go out the door and give you some time to yourself so you can figure out what's important to you. You really need to get your shit together before you lose the best thing that ever happened to you. I grabbed a pair of True Religion jeans and a white tank top out of our walk in closet and within minutes, I was out the door without the slightest clue as to where I was headed.

Jumping in my car, I immediately turned on the radio. I searched several stations until I heard my song "When a Woman's Fed Up" *by R. Kelly,* what a coincidence. Reaching in my tight ass jean pocket, I pulled out my cell phone. I called Buttah's and Sparkle's phone a couple of times and didn't get an answer from either. I cussed myself because I couldn't believe I was letting Nino get to me the way that he has. What goes around comes around is all I can say and he's definitely about to pay for all the shit he's been putting me through. I'm about to fuck his whole world up. He will never want to cheat on another bitch a day in his life once I'm through with him. After several attempts trying to get in contact with my girls, I decided to stop at a nearby IHOP to get something to eat.

$$$$$$$$$$

"Table for one please," I stated to the petite lady as I walked through the door.

Smiling, the hostess said, "Just give me a couple of minutes and I'll be right with you."

I walked outside and lit a cigarette to easy my mind. I couldn't believe I picked back up my old habit. I haven't smoked a cigarette in over three years. As mad as I was, I needed it or I was going to crack up. As I inhaled then exhaled the cigarette, my mind began to easy and my body felt more relax.

As soon as I walked back into the restaurant, the lady walked me to my table and told me my waiter will be with me shortly. Waiting patiently for my waiter to come, I noticed an older gentleman sitting at a table across from mine watching every move I made. He watched me like a hawk. Even though he was an older man, he had a young radiance about himself. I couldn't help, but to stare back because from where I was sitting he had it going on. He was a dark-skinned gentleman with salt and pepper hair and a neatly trimmed beard. Even though he was sitting down, I could tell that he was way over six-feet tall. The attire that he wore was strictly grown man gear. No gym shoes or jeans. Just the type of man I like.

Only a couple of minutes passed between us before he got up from his table and headed in my direction. The closer he got, the more attractive he became. I was a little nervous because I haven't interacted with any man besides Nino in four years.

"Are you waiting on another party?" He stated sounding like Berry White. His voice was so deep.

"No, I'm not." I stated in a flirtatious, but nervous voice. "I saw you over there watching me. Did your date stand you up?" Before he answered the question, he took a seat at my table without an invitation. I really needed the company so I didn't object to him sitting down.

"Nobody stood me up. I do breakfast by myself every morning. I believe everyone needs time to themselves whether it's doing the morning, late in the afternoon, or at night."

I huffed and puffed before replying, "I definitely understand what you're talking about."

"Is that why you are eating alone?" Now he's getting a little bit too nosey I thought to myself so I quickly changed the subject.

"All this time we've been talking I don't know your name"

"I do apologize for my rudeness; my name is Kane and yours"

"I'm Honeybun."

"So Honeybun, I see that you dodged the question, I threw at you. I'm only assuming that you are having a problem at home with your man that's why you're out having breakfast alone. I know you have a man because you're too beautiful not to have one. I'm not going to force you to answer the question, but I would love for you to listen to what I have to say."

"Go ahead I'm listening"

"Men are like night and day. We change quite often when we become comfortable with a person. I'm not saying that your man is tired of you, but you look like the type of female that use to run the street when you were younger and now that you have a man you became a home-body."

He paused for a minute then looked deep into my eyes as if he was reading my mind. "Please continue." I stated while looking at him with a smile upon my face. He just didn't know he was reading me like a book.

"When I say home-body, I don't mean you stay in the house 24/7. You still hang out with your girls from time to time, but you prefer to be with your man. You like that manly attention and you feel safe when you're with him."

Is this nigga psychic or what? Before he had a chance to continue to read me, the waiter came and interrupted and we placed our order. I couldn't do shit put shake my head because he was right on point.

We chatted for a while longer getting to know one another. I learned that he was single with four different baby mamas. I didn't give a fuck how many kids his old ass had. They were his problems not mine. I told him all about me, the good and the bad. I think I told him too much, but he listened attentively. We ate our breakfast then exchanged numbers. After he paid the tab, he walked me to my car. I thanked him for a nice breakfast, gave him a hug, and we parted ways. This might be a new beginning for me. I'm not looking for a man. I'm just looking to have some fun.

Chapter Ten
J-BOOGIE

*A*fter helping Buttah get rid of the body, of one of my sheisty workers, I had to call a meeting. Niggas were being disloyal to the crew and disrespecting my sister and I had to make sure that it never happened again. I wish she had left his ass breathing so I could have tortured his ass. Maybe cut off a couple of fingers and toes and set fire to his dick.

Everybody met up at my crib on time except Buttah. She said that she was running a little late so we just sat around talking and bullshitting until she got there. Didn't any of the other crewmembers know that K-Dub was dead? I wanted to read every nigga face in that room when I revealed to them he was breathless and if it looks like one of them had any knowledge that K-Dub was up to no good, I'm going to make an example out of his ass like Buttah did K-Dub.

I heard keys rattling at my door so I knew it was Buttah making her entrance.

"Settle down, settle down. Let's get this meeting started." I said while raising my voice just a little.

"Hey everybody," Buttah spoke as she made her way to take a seat on the couch.

All eyes were on her when she sat down. Her face was bruised and she walked with a slight limp. I hated she had to go through that shit with K-Dub and each time I see her in pain, I wish I could bring his ass back from the dead and kill his ass all over again.

Looking down at my watch I stated, "Do anybody know where K-Dub is at? It's seem like he's running late also."

"I tried calling him J, but I didn't get an answer," one of the guys stated and the other guys just shrugged their shoulders.

Clearing her throat Buttah begins to speak. "Well I know where he's at," while taking her gun out her purse and sitting it on her lap. Everyone had a strange, yet puzzling look on their face except one person. I didn't know what to make of it, but Gunz was one nigga that I definitely had to keep a close eye on. Even though he's been a part of the team for a while, I trusted no man.

"Where the nigga at, baby sis?" I stated, while still keeping a close eye on the four niggas that occupied my apartment, but a closer eye on Gunz."

"That snake ass nigga is dead."

"Dead; what you mean he's dead?" One of the little niggas jumped up and shouted out.

"Do I need to spell the motherfucking word out for you? D-E-A-D-dead, nigga." His bitch ass raped me and tried to rob me, so I had to show him that I was one bitch that can't be fucked with. He thought it was sweet because I have a split between my legs, but I come from a family of lions, tigers, and bears and I wasn't going down without a fight.

Clearing his throat, Gunz spoke up, "He's one less nigga we have to worry about, which means more money in my pocket; so, let's get money."

I didn't know what to make of the response, so I just smiled and replied, "Let's get money. The purpose of this meeting is to let you niggas know that the type of shit K-Dub pulled will not be tolerated under any circumstances; we all in this for the same reason. There's no room for backstabbers and definitely no room for snitches. If we live by those two rules, we all will get along just fine, but the moment one of those rules are broken, be prepared to die. There's no need to get greedy because there is enough money to go around. Are we all on the same page?"

In unison, everyone spoke, "Yea, we all on the same page."

"That's all I needed to hear; meeting adjourned."

$$SSSSSSSS$$

Every major hustler from Chicago was in the

building, including that nigga Dough-Boy. He had really been getting out more lately. Every time I see him, I
just want to walk up to him and rob his ass off GP because he thinks he's untouchable. He walks around
with nothing less than 10 racks in his pocket and thinks
a nigga like me won't rob his ass. He better think again.
Every time I see him, he has an entourage with him, but
I'm not going to let that stop me. Dough-Boy is definitely on my hit list, but I know I have to take a different
approach with him. I can't follow him around like them
other cats without getting caught and I can't throw
pussy in his face because he gets plenty of it. Oh yea, I
have my work cut out with this one, but I know it will
be worth it. I've noticed that he has the same three guys
with him at all times. I might have to cut one of them in
on the deal.

Leaning on the bar, glancing out into the crowd
of people that had the party pack to its capacity, I decided that I wasn't going to put any work in tonight so I
bobbed my head to the music while sipping on a cup of
yack.

"Nigga, you better watch what the fuck you doing," I snapped immediately after some nigga bumped
me causing me to drop my drink.

"Nigga, I don't have to watch shit. He stated
firmly. "You don't remember me do you?" Dude stated
as he walked in my face not breaking eye contact with
me.

Looking closely, I noticed that it was a local,

'hood-rich nigga named Dee-Man that I got at a couple of weeks ago just to prove a point to his stunting ass.

"Where the fuck is my money?" He shouted over the loud music.

"Money! What money? Dude I don't know what you talking about," I stated as I stared him directly in his eyes not blinking once.

"I know you and your crew hit me. K-Dub told me all about it." *This snitch ass nigga. I'm glad Buttah did kill his sheisty ass.*

"Like I told you before, I don't know what you talking about, homie, so you better get out my face before you get into some shit that you won't be able to get out." Trying not to cause a big uproar I walked away, but Dee-Man rushed me from behind. I flipped him over my shoulder causing him to land on a table, pulled my gun out my waistline, and pointed it in his face. "Listen here, li'l nigga, this is not what your nut ass looking for."

"Nigga, if you don't kill me, you better believe I'm gonna kill you," he shouted. I'm far from a fool, so I had to be a playa about the situation. There were too many witnesses so I knew I had to get at Dee-Man another time. Therefore, I politely told him, "I'll see you in the streets my nigga."

Chapter Eleven
NINO

"**P**ut your hands on the steering wheel," the police shouted as his words shivered out his
mouth, after pulling me over. *What the fuck I
do now?* I asked myself. I guess it's just another case of
'driving while black.'

"What's the problem, Mr. Officer," I shouted,
angrily.

"License and insurance, please," he stated in a
calm voice, his hand on his gun, ready to shoot my ass if
I made the wrong move.

"Officer, I'm not handing you shit until you tell
me why you pulled me over." I could tell he was a rookie. I saw fear written all across his face, so I took advantage of the moment.

"Sir, you have a busted tail light," he shouted.

"Busted tail light?" *That bitch Honeybun.* "You have to be kidding me. Just write me a ticket, so I can go."

"Sir, I'm afraid it's not that easy, but can you please give me your license and insurance?" He stated again, calmly. His hand never left his gun, so I handed him my license and insurance card because I didn't want his finger to get an itch that needed to be scratched.

While he was running my name through the system, I quickly retrieved my gun from my waist and hid it in a secret compartment that I had built in my car for times like these. I sat in my car singing out loud, "Fuck the Police."

Gun now drawn in my face, "Mr. Rayfield, I need you to step out the car; there is a warrant for your arrest."

"Warrant, what the fuck you talking 'bout? I haven't did shit to have a warrant. This has to be a fucking mistake."

"If this is a mistake, we can clear things up at the police station. Now get out the car and put your hands on top of your head."

Sitting in this cold, nasty ass cell had me thinking about Honeybun. I'm definitely going to beat her ass for busting my tail light; that's a given. She knows that I don't play about my cars. I also was trying to decide when I was going to let her know that I was leaving her. I don't blame her for being upset with me. I must admit I have been a total jerk. I do know if the shoe was on the other foot, I'll be acting the same way. I use to cover up my cheating ways, but lately I have this I don't give a fuck attitude. Even though I've been with Honeybun for years, I think it time we go our separate ways. I've lost interest in her. I'm not attractive to her anymore. Between her and my new lover, she's the weakest link. Being in her presence aggravates me. That's why I choose to stay away from her as much as possible. I know I'm hurting her, so sooner or later I'm going to come clean with her. Every time I look at her beautiful face, I see the hurt in her eyes. Even though she has been with me through thick and thin, according to the heart her time is up. The only reason why I haven't come clean with her just yet is because I'm trying to make sure that I'm making the right choice with my newfound love. I love Honeybun to death, but only as a friend. She deserves so much better than me. I know in due time she will find that special man that can love her the way that she deserve to be love because she is a good woman, and she has proven that to me time and time again. I hope my new girl doesn't let me down. Boo better be worth all the pain and heartache I'm taking Honeybun through.

"Rayfield, you are being released. Let's go."

After calling my lawyer, everything was cleared up. Those whack ass cops was trying to charge me with murder. The police had made a mistake. I wasn't going down for any murder I didn't commit. That stupid ass rookie cop had got my named mixed up. There was a warrant for a Nino Rayford, not Nino Rayfield.

$$$$$$$$

Walking out the police station a free man, I headed straight to the hood to check on my workers and my money. My day had already started wrong and I hate to pull up and these little niggas are not on point.

Pulling up, I yelled, "Yo, Dre, didn't I tell your tall, lanky ass to stop selling those bootlegged CDs and DVDs on this corner? Sell that shit around the corner or up the street somewhere." Dre stared at me as if I wasn't speaking to him or if I was speaking to him in another language, so I jumped out my black 745 with peanut interior and walked toward him while balling up my fist and pounding it into the palm of my other hand.

"Nino, I'm just trying to get my hustle on like you. Why you gotta knock my hustle?"

"Ain't nobody knockin' your hustle. My block is already hot and you're making it hotter by selling more illegal shit. This corner is only made for selling weed, dope, and crack, so take your nickel and dime hustling ass elsewhere," I yelled.

I know I was being a little hard on him and I know he has to eat, too, but I can't have that type of hustling on my corner. Moreover, I was frustrated because I didn't see any of my people posted up. These niggas was making me lose money and that was something that I just couldn't tolerate.

Three cluckas walked up, looking dope sick. "Yo, homey," I shouted, not speaking to anyone in particular, "Give me 10 minutes. Walk around the block or up the street and when y'all come back my man will set y'all straight."

One of the cluckas looked at me and smiled with his rotten teeth. I know I have good products, so I knew they were definitely coming back. I drove around a couple of blocks looking for my workers, but they were nowhere in sight so I decided to head back to the block. When I arrived, all three of them were posted up with their lady friends. How many times do I have to tell these young punks money over pussy? Money rule the world not bitches. When I pulled up, I called Twon's name and he headed to the car. He saw the look I had on my face, and before I had a chance to asked him where they been he shouted out, "Boss man we went to the restaurant. We were hungry. We were only gone for about ten minutes."

I looked him dead in his eye and told him "next time starve nigga. Time is money and if I miss out on money, I'm gonna kick somebody ass, and we don't want that to happen, now do we?" Twon shook his head from side to side to indicate no.

"I don't understand head shaking language, li'l nigga. Use your motherfucking mouth boy."

"Noooooo, boss man, we don't want that to happen."

"Now take your ass back over there and inform

the others of our conversation and next time y'all get hungry send them hood rats y'all consider women to the restaurant."

I know I was being tough on my workers, but if they wanted to survive in the game, they need to realize that money come before pleasure. No bitch should distract them from getting money, not even their mommas. There are rules to this shit and it's very simple. Money first and everything else comes after.

As Twon skipped his short, round body back to the others, my cell phone began to ring.

"What up, boo," I sang into my cell phone, when I noticed her phone number flash across the screen.

"Nothing at all, sweetheart, I just wanted to know what time you were coming over so I can have dinner hot and ready for you once you walk through the door. I also have this special dessert that I prepared for you and I know you gonna love it."

"Special dessert...huh," I said, and then smiled to myself. "I'll be there in about two hours. That should give you enough time to prepare what you have in store for me."

"Okay, love ya."

"Love ya, too, and by the way, put on those sexy red pumps I bought you the other day." I felt kind of bad knowing that I had a woman at home and I'm telling another person I love them. Honestly, I have to do what makes me happy and being with my newfound

love is what makes me happy. I guess Honeybun will
have another lonely night to herself.

Chapter Twelve
SPARKLE

*T*he air in my apartment had the aroma of fingernail remover and fingernail polish. I patiently gave myself a manicure and pedicure because I didn't feel like being bother with them chinks today. It's hot as hell outside and I know they are going to be crowded with all the local chicken heads.

Watching "Paid in Full" on my 52' high definition TV had me laughing hysterically, while waiting for my nails and toes to dry. Even though I tried to stay busy, Bone continued to invade my mind and I was fighting to keep him out of it. I had a lot of mixed emotions about him at this point.

Hopping off the couch, I headed to the bathroom to take a warm shower to easy my mind. As the water stimulated my clitoris, my head fell back in enjoyment, imagining that it was Bone pleasing me.

After I showered, I lotion my body up with some Japanese Cherry Blossom lotion that I bought from Bath -N- Body Works a couple days prior. Rubbing the lotion over my skin made my skin glow. I got dressed and headed to my girl Juicy's house to see what she was doing for the day. Riding down Ohio I waved to the hood celebrities as they stood on the corner getting their hustle on.

Zigzagging through traffic, doing 50mph in a 30mph zone, I found myself halfway to her house within minutes. Bobbing my head to the music, I continued to drive at a speedy pace without a care in the world. Looking to the right of me and then to the left, I noticed a lot of people hanging out enjoying the nice weather. While all the chicks stood in position and scoped out their next victim, I continue on my journey to Juicy's house to find out the latest gossip.

Just a block away from her house, the unthinkable happened. A loud crashing sound invaded my ears. My body jerked forward as I hit the side of an all-black car with tinted windows. The black car looked familiar, but I blew it off because my main concern was to see if the individual that I just hit was okay. For a moment, we both just sat in our car. I guess we both were in shock about the accident. I hit the side of the car hard, leaving a huge dent in the driver and backseat door. I could only imagine what the front of my car look like. I saw a familiar figure exit the car as I continued to sit in my car staring at the person in front of me. He was too busy looking at the dent to notice it was me who hit him. Yes, the accident was my fault. I ran the stop sign while looking in my mirror and applying MAC lip-gloss to my lips. What was even more fucked up was a couple of seconds later I saw Buttah exiting the car. The first thing that came to mind was that she was at it again.

"Look at my damn car," Bone shouted loudly.

I exited my vehicle pissed off, but I showed no emotions and stated, "I do apologize, sir. Just give me your information and I will have my insurance company take care of everything."

He turned his head around at the sound of my voice and his eyes grew as big as his head when he laid his eyes on me. I acted like I didn't even see Buttah standing there. She had her head held high as usual, like she was God's gift to the world. She stood there and spoke to me like she just didn't get out of his car. When she spoke, it fell on deaf ears.

"There's no need, Sparkle, the dent isn't that bad. I can take care of it myself," Bone state with a guilty voice.

I stood there trying to hold my composure, but out of nowhere, I snapped. "Damn right you will take care of it you piece of shit."

"Calm down, shawty, what's your motherfucking problem? You're the one that hit me. I should be the one pissed."

"Bone, don't play stupid with me. What is this bitch doing in your car?" Not giving him a chance to answer I continued, "Let me guess y'all fucking. You can fuck anybody in the world, but what I do not understand is why you would fuck with my girl."

"Hold on one motherfucking minute. First of all, who the fuck you calling a bitch? I got your bitch, bitch. You need to calm down 'cause I'm not gonna listen to these false accusations about me. Nobody is fucking your li'l boyfriend, sweetheart." Taking a deep breathe Buttah continue with a much calmer voice. Listen Sparkle, we don't mess around," she said pointing at him then back at herself. "He saw me stranded down the street with a flat tire. He pulled over and asked me if I needed help. I told him yes. Then he offered to take me to my apartment to get my spare tire because I don't keep it in my truck."

Sounds like a bunch of bullshit to me. Who does this bitch think she's talking to, Boo-Boo the Fool. I didn't respond to her because she was only doing what Buttah does best. I knew I wasn't Bone's woman, but it was the principle that counted. I would never do the things to Buttah that she had done to me. She knew how I felt about him and she still gave him the pussy. Females like her never have any luck. I know she had sex with him because that's her character, but this one time I'm going to give her the benefit of the doubt. If I find out anything different, I'm going to tear both of their heads off.

I didn't care to stand there any longer to entertain them two so I took a quick glance at the front end of my car, cursed out loud, jumped in my vehicle, and continued to my destination. Of course, I was still heated about seeing them two together. I wasn't worried about the damage to the front end of my car at all because Bone was going to take care of me and his damages. I wasn't going to notify my insurance company at all. I called both of them every name that I could think of as I continued on my journey to Juicy's house, but made a quick detour to the weed spot and the liquor store.

When I arrived on Juicy's block, the ambulance and several police cars were on her block. It wasn't anything new to me because she lived in Afghanistan; this is what we called the south side of Chicago.

"What up Sparkle," She shouted from her porch as I excited my car.

"Hey chic it's been a long time since I've stopped over this way. I see ain't nothing change about your block, but the number of shootouts.

Before I got a chance to tell her about the accident, she yelled out, "What happened to your car."

"Girl let's go inside under AC and I'll tell you all about it."

To my surprise when I got in her house, her baby daddy Dee-Man was there. At that time of the day, he normally is out checking some paper. I spoke and sat down on the couch. I pulled out my weed, grabbed my blunt out my purse, and told Juicy to go grab us some cups so we could enjoy this fifth of Patron.

We all sat around getting high, tipsy, and talking shit. I told them about the car accident and the fact that I think Bone and Buttah were fucking. I noticed Juicy's words becoming slurred. She wasn't a drinker and every time Juicy gets high, she gets sleepy that why I shouldn't have given her that shit. The mixture of the liquor and weed had her knocked out in a matter of minutes.

Dee-Man kept eyeing me from across the room and touching his crotch. He was a short sexy caramel complexion nigga with a played out curly kit in his head. I tried to ignore his stares, but the mixture of the liquor and the weed had my pussy on fire. I was sexually deprived because of Bone. I glanced over to make sure Juicy was still knocked out and she was. I called her name, but she didn't answer so that gave me the green light to do what my body wanted to do and my mind was telling me not to do. Still upset about seeing Bone and Buttah together, I took my built up frustration out on Juicy. I walked over, grabbed Dee-Man's hand, and lead him into her bedroom.

Drunk and high sex is the best sex. He was tearing this pussy up. In the midst of us having sex, I kept telling Dee-Man I was hearing noise. For a moment, I thought Juicy had awakened. He told me I was tripping. Maybe he was right so I blew it off, blamed it on me being intoxicated, and kept at the task at hand. I was riding his dick like it was the last dick on earth and I relished every moment of it. It's was hard trying to keep myself under composure. The sex was feeling so good to me. The drug and the liquor had my body out of control. Not having a care in the world, I continued to ride his dick like he was my man.

Bam!

As the closed door gets kicked in, I jumped off of Dee-man's dick and retreat under the cover. I was so embarrassed that Juicy had caught us.

Pop! Pop! Pop! Just like that, Dee-Man was dead. I screamed out in fear, I yelled out, "I'm sorry Juicy please don't kill me," but I never got a response. Too scared to look Juicy in her face, I just laid there under the cover while Dee-man's dead body lay next to me.

"What the fuck," is all I heard Juicy say.

"I'm sorry Juicy, please forgive me." I said still under the cover. I couldn't believe that Juicy killed Dee-Man and I know if she killed him that easily I was next. I regret putting myself in this situation.

As the cover gets snatched off my body, the cold air rushed my skin giving me goose pumps. Scared out my mind, I screamed out again, with my eyes closed, "I'm sorry."

"Bitch shut up and get over there before I kill you," I heard a voice say, but it wasn't Juicy's voice that I heard that echoed throughout the room.

Now I'm scared shitless because my life is in a total stranger's hands. When I opened my eyes the gunman had the gun pointed in Juicy's direction and he told her not to say another word and sit down next to me. With tears streaming down her face, she followed suit. Even though I saw fear in her eyes, I also saw a look of hatred in her eyes toward me after she glanced at my naked body then at her dead baby daddy's naked body.

The gunman came over, pushed Dee-Man's body on the floor, and yelled out, "nigga I told you, I'll see you in the streets, but in this case your home." The gunman laughed a wicked laugh then politely walked out of the room leaving me and Juicy alive.

Chapter Thirteen
BUTTAH

*O*ear Buttah,

I know I can be a sucka at times, but I woke up this morning and felt like this needed to be said. For a long time, I thought me being happy and falling in love wasn't possible until I met you. When I was in the streets, you gave me hope again and you gave me a reason to smile. I don't know what it is about you, but you make my heart beat a certain way. I'm not gonna question the big man upstairs, but I thank him from the bottom of my heart for giving me the opportunity to be a part of your life. Sometimes I sit and think about my situation, but don't ponder on it to long because I'll be in here for the rest of my life. I've been through a lot and through it all, you have been right here by my side. You're my ride or die chic and will always be. I'm not trying to spark up old memories, but you were on my mind and I just want to drop you a couple of lines.

Love Always, Killa

P.S. When you come back to visit me tell J-Boogie to come holla at me also because I gotta tell him something that's going to definitely put a smile on his face and don't forget to bring my 50yr old grand-daddy as well.

After reading the letter from Killa, I placed it against my heart. I closed my eyes for a brief moment and thought about all the good times we shared. I must admit, I really do miss him and he is right, I will always be his ride or die chick. I still visit him and take care of him because I owe him. He made sure I lived a very comfortable life before he got locked up. Once a person earns my loyalty, they have it for life.

Several weeks has passed since K-Dub raped me and now I'm back to my old self again. Relaxing in a tub full of bubbles, all that clouded my mind was money and who the next victim was going to be. Even though K-Dub did what he did to me, thanks to him, I'm a stronger and more alert person. I never really had any feelings, when it came to robbing these niggas, but now my body is numb and nothing pumps through my veins but ice. I'm showing these niggas we rob no mercy. If they play with the whereabouts of the money, it's rock a bye baby.

Growing up, I didn't have these conniving ways. Actually, I was a straightforward, respectable, non-troublemaking kid. As I became a teenager, I noticed my oldest cousin bring money in like it grew on trees. That alone made me fiend for some excitement in my boring life. The moment she told me how she got her money I knew I wanted in. I knew if she could bring money in by spreading her legs, I knew I could do the same. My cousin was an average looking chic, but with a banging body and me on the other hand had the looks to go along with the banging body. She tried to keep me away from the negativity the streets had to offer and her hoe-ish ways. She knew that no matter how bad she didn't want me to follow her example; I made my own decisions so she showed me the ropes without giving it a second thought. Throughout it all, I still graduated from college to make my mother proud. When my mom meet J-Boogie father and she introduced me to my soon to be stepbrother at the time, he turn me on to his hustle immediately and after that it was all she wrote.

Feeling so fresh and so clean, I threw on something comfortable to go meet Honeybun and Sparkle for brunch. With all that has been going on, I haven't really had much time to spend with them.

Walking into the restaurant, which sat in the middle of the hood, I noticed that Honeybun and Sparkle was already sitting and waiting patiently at the table for me. Normally, I am the early one and they are the late ones. The food was just coming out when I arrived. We all order the same thing every time we come so they already order my food upon my arrival.

"Hey, what's up, my bitches? I miss y'all," meaning every word that I spoke. It felt good being in their presence.

"Awww…we miss you, too, Buttah," Honeybun spoke, as she stood up and gave me a hug.

"Yea, we really do miss you Buttah," Sparkle stated sarcastically, but I blew it off.

"Buttah you be so busy you don't have time for your girls no more what's up with that," Honeybun stated.

"You know it's not like that girl. These niggas be taking up all my time. You know I have bills that have to be paid and I'm not letting anything or anyone come between my money, not even you bitches." Laughter broke out from everyone at the table.

"I feel you," Sparkle stated sarcastically again. "Make that money, don't let it make you."

Sparkle and her sarcastic ways wasn't bothering me one bit. I acted like I didn't even noticed how she was acting. I was just happy to be in the presence of my girls despite what Sparkle may have thought about me at the time. We sat in the restaurant for about an hour enjoying each other company. We talked about everything that came to mind. We all agreed to hit the club this upcoming weekend. We haven't hung out since that incident that occurred with Sheena. I love my bitches so I'm going to make sure I show them a good time when we hang out.

$$$$$$$$$

The weekend had come and left and I really enjoyed the company of my girls, but it was time out for fun and back to business as usual. I spoke with J-Boogie briefly and he told me that within a week, I'll be flying out to North Carolina for our next target. I was excited because I had an old friend there that I meet a while back while I was vacationing in Virginia and it would feel good to see him. The last time Derrell and I spoke, he and his baby mama were breaking up. She was some video vixen that didn't know how not to mix business with pleasure. According to him, some random guy walked up to him on the streets and handed him a DVD of her having sex with ten men. He said at first he didn't know what to think of the DVD dude handed him and he wanted to throw it away, but all that kept playing in his head was dude stressing for him to watch what he gave him and under no circumstance for him to throw it away.

The day he received the movie he was on his way to the barbershop. He asked his barber to throw it in the player and when he did; his heart sank to his stomach when he saw what was in front of him. Even though he did him from time to time, he really was in love with his baby mama, but he couldn't get past what he saw on that DVD.

Calling Derrell, I told him that I'd be in town within a week so clear his schedule for me. I could have easily robbed him, but his southern hospitality did something to me so I refuse to set him up.

$$\mathscr{SSSSSSSS}$$

Landing in Charlotte I had excitement running all through my body. I was excited about spending time with Derrell. I phoned him and told him once I settle in I'll be to see him.

Walking through the airport, I was greeted by two of my brother's workers. They arrived in Charlotte a day prior to me. We immediately headed to the hotel and got right down to business. We discussed the details of who we were setting up. The person's name was C-Lo and he was bringing in a lot of cash in the south. Our plan was to go into action the next day so in the mean time I was going to spend some time with Derrell. I made sure I went over to his crib with the shortest skirt that I had in my luggage. I wanted him to have easy access.

Meeting up with Derrell at his house had me feeling like a schoolgirl falling in love at first sight. If we didn't live so far away from each other, I could have very well seen us together long term.

"Hey sexy lady," he stated as he greeted me with a hug after I knocked on his door.

"Hey Derrell," I responded while wrapping my arms around him not wanting to let go.

Breaking the embrace, he looked me up and down and shouted, "Damn, shawty, it's been a long time since the last time I've laid eyes on you and you sexier than a motherfucka."

"Yea, it has been a minute." I replied as I walked into his apartment and giggled a little.

Sitting down on his couch, enjoying each other's company, he tongued-kissed my neck and my panties got wet instantly. His hands went up my mini skirt and his finger went in and out of my pussy soaking up my juices. I haven't been with him in a long time so there definitely was no need for talking. I wanted him right then and there.

Knock! Knock! Knock!

Bam! Bam! Bam!

Our intimate moment was interrupted and I became annoyed by the loud knocks coming from the door.

"Who the hell could this be," Derrell stated as he got up off the couch and headed toward the door to see who was on the other side. As he peeped through his peephole, he shook his head. I just sat on the couch waiting patiently so I could see who was on the other side of the door. Whoever it was they were pissed off about something.

After he opened up the door, his baby momma storm through the door with a diaper bag and their son. I continue to sit there to see what was going to be the outcome of this situation.

"Derrell, I know you seen me calling your phone. You know I have a video shoot today so why you playing with me."

"Aisha, I told you yesterday that I wasn't going to watch him because I had some business to attend to today."

She looked in my direction and pointed at me and screamed, "You call fucking some hoe business, nigga I got money to make so take this baby 'cause I have to go."

Aisha was a none-motherfucking factor so I didn't even feed into her bullshit. Without saying another word, she stormed out the door leaving Derrell standing there with a diaper bag in his hand and his son smelling like a bag of shit. What I don't do is kids or drama so I had to get up out of there.

I was saved by Beyoncé as she sang through my phone. I didn't know what excuse I was going to use before my phone rung, but all praises to my brother for ringing my line. I chatted with my brother for a minute and told Derrell that I had to go. I politely got off the couch, grabbed my purse, and headed out the door. I had no attentions of seeing Derrell ever again because I can't stand a nigga that don't have their baby momma under control.

$$$$$$$$$

It was 10:30 p.m. when my date decided to pick me up. I stood in front of my hotel waiting patiently for him. As the dry heat blew in my direction, a sense of embarrassment took over me when C-Lo came pulling up blasting his music in the quite area the hotel was located in. As people stared at us, I jumped in the car and immediately turned down the radio. Before speaking, he turned in my direction and kissed me on the cheek then we pulled off.

"How you doing this beautiful night," he spoke breath smelling like straight liquor.

"I'm doing okay, can't complain now that I'm in your presence."

"That what's up, shorty, now where you say yo' sexy ass from again," C-Lo stated, as he rubbed his fingers through my hair.

I ran into C-Lo earlier that day at the carwash that he owned. I was getting my rental car washed and cleaned out. It was hard trying to get his attention because the half-naked females that he employed to wash the cars were entertaining him. Walking back and forward past him wasn't doing the job so I accidently bumped one of the females carrying a bucket of water. As the water wet the whole top portion of my body, it gave him a good view of my breasts in my white shirt. While fussing and cursing, he came over, offered his apology for his clumsy worker, and offered to take me out later in the day. We decided we would go to a park and have a nice picnic for our first date.

"All that doesn't matter. All that matter is we here getting to know one another," I spoke as the hot air blew through the car windows on this steamy summer night.

As we drove through a couple of unfamiliar blocks I looked through the rearview mirror to make sure Marty had a close tail on us and he did. I'm glad he wasn't too close to make things look suspicious. When the car stopped, we were in front of an abandon looking house. He jumped out the car and said he will be back in a minute. I immediately texted Marty and Gunz told them we should be heading to the park after this so get ready.

When C-Lo jumped back in the car, he had a suitcase handcuffed to his wrist. I knew now, he had attached to him what we had come for. At this point, the only thing that was on my mind was money and getting the hell out of North Carolina. The game plan was to kidnap him and make him take us to where the money was at, but he was making it too easy for us. Easing from the curb, we continued on our journey.

"Baby, did I tell you how hot you look?"

"No, but I'm all ears," I spoke with a smile on my face.

"Girl, you are a heartbreaker," he tried flattering me while taking his eyes off the road.

"Hit the brakes. Hit the brakes," I screamed out as we drove down a dark secluded block.

Coming to a quick stop our head jerked back and forth like a bobble head. I jumped out the car to assist the old man that was lying in the middle of the street that C-Lo almost ran over.

"Get back in the car Buttah; I got some serious

business to take care of. Whoever that is on the ground is the least of my concern."

"Come here C-Lo, we can't leave this old man in the middle of the street like this." Putting my hand to check his pulse," I yelled he's not breathing.

"So leave his dead ass alone."

"The least we can do is get him out the street so nobody can run him over like you almost did and call the police. Please C-Lo, have a fucking heart. Help me with this old man. I know you got business to take care of. This will only take a quick moment."

"Girl, if you weren't sexy, I would leave you and that old ass man right where y'all at.

When C-Lo jumped out his car, he still had that suitcase handcuffed to his wrist. I was anticipating on him having it off. Any way it goes, we were getting what was in that suitcase.

"Grab his feet, while I grab his upper body," C-Lo instructed.

"Wait a minute," I stated as I ran back toward the car.

"Where the fuck are you going?" His eyes followed me back to the car.

"Give me the suitcase," Gunz stated, as he got off the ground and point the .38 caliber to the back of C-Lo head while wiping the makeup off his face with his other hand.

"Come on now, what you trying to do rob a nigga?"

"Trying isn't the word nigga, you are about to get robbed."

"You have a choice. Give me the suitcase or get your wrist sawed off; either way, what's in that suitcase is mines," I stated now, letting him know I was in on everything.

"I don't know the passcode to get inside. The person I was going to meet knows the code.

"Do you think we're stupid?" I stated, taking over the whole situation. Gunz just watched as I handled my business.

As Marty pulled up, I told him to pop the trunk. I walked to the back of the truck and retrieved a saw. There was no time to waste. Even though we were in that secluded area, there was no telling when another car will be coming past.

"I'm only going to say it one more time. Now it's your call. You can either give up the code to the suitcase or give us your wrist."

My cell phone began to vibrate. When I looked down, it was a text message that was marked urgent. The message was coming from some chick J-Boogie fucked from time to time when he came to NC. The text read, 'here comes one.'

"Put the nigga in the car. There's a vehicle coming our way."

"Move your feet, motherfucker, move," Gunz stated, as he kept aim with the .38 caliber at C-Lo's head.

I ran and opened the back door and the two jumped in the back seat. Just as I jumped in the front seat of the car, a white Bentley cruised by us. We locked eyes and all I could do was shake my head. The Bentley came to a stop and I told Gunz to pull off. All I heard Derrell say was, "Buttah, what the fuck y'all doing with my cousin?"

"Shit, shit, shit," I cursed repeatedly, as I hit the side of my fist against the window.

"Derrell is your cousin, C-Lo?"

"How the fuck you know my cousin?"

"It's doesn't matter how I know your cousin."

"Well, since you know him, give him a call and tell him to give you the code 'cause he's the one I was going to meet."

"We don't need to do all of that. There is only one way this scene is going to be played out."

Chapter Fourteen
HONEYBUN

Kane has really been showing me a lot of attention and I love every bit of it. I haven't had this type of attention from a man in a long time. Kane and I hang out with each other every other day. He's such a perfect gentleman and when I say "perfect gentleman" I mean it in the full context. He opens doors for me, cooks for me, showers me with gifts, and on top of that he never asked to sleep with me. I asked him one day over breakfast why he never made a move on me, and he simply stated because he don't want to rush things between us. I couldn't do nothing, but respect his answer. It really made me feel good because I'm used to men wanting to jump all over my bones. Whenever I'm in Kane's presence Nino is the last thing on my mind. It feels like I'm living in a fantasy world when I'm with him. He's just too good to be true. If I had known what I know now, I would have started dating older men a long time ago. It seems like I've known him forever because it feels like he knows everything about me before I tell him. Even though he's a perfect gentleman, I still have needs that need to be met because my man isn't doing his job. Therefore, the times I'm not fussing with Nino or being wined and dined by Kane, I'm out doing my thing.

$$SSSSSSSS$$

"A different day, another trick," I said, underneath my breath, as I rolled out of bed with...ummm, ummm, damn, I can't even remember his name. His name is not what's important. What's important is how I straddled his dick and rode $500 out of him. The moment he entered my love tunnel I knew he never experience pussy like this before. I had the nigga screaming my name and scratching my back. I really was putting it on his young ass. He was an 18 year-old money machine. I knew he was used to fucking with teenyboppers and he wasn't used to getting this type of grown woman pussy.

The whole time I was riding dude, I pictured him being Kane. I wish Kane would let me please him the way dude did. I really do find it attractive that a man is making me wait, but damn if Kane not sleeping with me I wonder who he is sleeping with. After a couple more good strokes dude busted a nut. I jumped off his dick and looked at it to make sure the condom was still in place, and it was. I'm glad it was in place because there was no room for mistakes. I grabbed my pay, walked out of the expensive hotel, and left dude with a big Kool-Aid smile on his face. I jumped in my car and headed home to a place I considered hell.

$$$$$$$$$

Nino hasn't been home in a couple of days and it's not bothering me one bit. I even took the initiative of packing his things and changing the locks. Even though I love him, I'm not a fool for love. I'm not new to the game; I'm true to the game. I'm not going to sit back and let him come and go as he pleases. I'll be less of a woman if I allow that to happen. I refuse to let him continue to hurt me. I stood by his side when times were ruff and this is how he repays me. When he went to jail, I was the one who held the streets down for him. I was the one to make sure his street operations ran smoothly not his so-called right hand man. When he went to jail, I was the one there bonding him out, not them hoes he cheats on me with. So you see, I can be that classy chick, but when it's time to hold it down for my nigga, I can be his gangsta bitch.

Leaving the bank, I cleaned out me and Nino's joint account. I cleaned that one out first because he almost never withdraws money from it. The total was $105, 285.14. When I withdrew our money, I mean, MY money, the branch manager asked if everything was all right. I smiled and simply told her everything is

fine and the money was going to buy me a new beginning. She had a look on her face that read she wanted to
ask another question, but she didn't. I left out the bank
without a care in the world.

Withdrawing the money really gave me hope
for a new beginning. Money really can't buy me happiness, but it can definitely buy me a lot of other shit. I
guess I'll treat myself to a new purse today I thought
while recounting the money in my car under tinted
windows. My plans were falling through smoothly so
far. I put an ad in the newspaper to sell two of his cars.
Once I sell those two then I'll post the others. I chose the
newspaper for two reasons. One, because it reaches
millions in a matter of minutes and two, because I
didn't want to get any of the local 'hood boys' business;
they're too stupid to pick up the newspaper to read.
Half of them boys dropped out of school in the eighth
grade so reading somebody's newspaper was the last
thing on their minds. I also met with my realtor and my
house is now on the market. Hopefully, that will be sold
soon.

For a minute, I started to second-guess what I
was doing. I knew once Nino found out I was robbing
him the consequences that came behind that was death.
Then I thought, his cheating no good ass deserves everything that he got coming his way. I didn't plan on
getting caught and by the time, he found out that I took
him for everything I planned to be long gone.

$$$$$$$$$

Tuesday morning, I was awakened by loud bangs and kicks at my front door. I knew it could only be one person, which was Nino. I knew he was going to have a fit once he put his key in the door and it didn't work. I let him stay on the other side of the door for a couple minutes until he started screaming my name. I got up off the couch, a place I slept on a regular, with an attitude because I just walked in the house two hours prior.

"Damn, here I come." I shouted from the other side of my door.

"Bitch, I'm going to beat your ass once I get in this house and why in the hell did you change the damn locks?"

"Just for that threat nigga, you won't be getting in at all."

Still banging on the door, Nino screamed, "Bitch, I'm not playing with you, open the fucking door, Heidi."

"Stay your good for nothing ass out there. I changed the locks 'cause you don't live here. As a matter of fact, take your ass back to where you been for the last couple of days."

I guess what I was saying to him didn't matter because he continued kicking and beating on the door. I looked out the window and noticed our neighbors coming out of their houses to see what the big commotion was all about. *White folks and the suburbs.* People can be so damn nosey at times. I didn't want everybody in our business so I let his sorry ass in.

As soon as he got through the door, he started swinging and I started ducking. What he had to know was that I wasn't taking any more ass whippings without a fight. I was not going to just stand there like the old days and accept a beating. Today the roles were reversed. I was Ike and he was Tina. I finally built up enough courage and picked up the bat that I had lying on the side of the couch and hit his ass a couple of times with it. It felt so good being in control. I hit his ass about seven good times before he got hold of the bat. He jerked it out of my hand and tossed it across the room breaking a lamp. Immediately, I went in panic mode. I scanned the room quickly looking for something else to hit him with, but didn't see anything that could possible cause bodily harm. He began to walk toward me and I began to run around the couch. I was determined not to let him catch me. Still trying to decide what my next move was going to be, I quickly remember that I've been sleeping with a knife under my pillow anticipating this day. Reaching for the pillow and throwing it in his face, I got hold of the knife and charged at him. He started screaming. That's when I knew that the knife had made contact with his skin. He finally got a taste of what it felt like to be defeated. I ran to the kitchen and grabbed a bottle of disinfected spray from under the sink. I sprayed his ass a couple of times causing his opened wounds to burn. "I'm gonna kill you, bitch," he screamed out. "Not before I kill you, motherfucka." I shouted back. He continued to scream, but much louder. If one of our nosey neighbors wouldn't have knocked on our cracked door and asked if everything was all right, I would have caught a murder case. I had so much anger in me. I walked to the front door and told the neighbor to mind his fucking business then slam the door in his face.

As Tom walked off my property, I turned around with the knife still in my hand ready to continue to slice his ass into little bitty pieces. As I looked at Nino, he was standing there like a little girl with one single tear rolling down his cheek. I finally defeated him. I bet he won't ever raise his hands at me again.

I spoke softly to him through closed teeth and said, "Nino, your bags are awaiting you in the closet behind the front door. All that's missing is the rightful owner to carry them out."

He had a pitiful look on his face. I felt kind of sorry for him for a couple of seconds. I was even contemplating on letting him stay, but I knew that once I did that, things were going to be great for about a month, then right back down the road to destruction.

"What are you talking about? You can't put me out. This is my house."

"If I recall correctly, my name is on this house not yours so if you would be so kind to grab your things and leave I would greatly appreciate it."

"I don't care if your name is on this house or not. My hard-earned money is what paid for this house, not yours. Honeybun, I'm not going anywhere. I pay all the bills."

"Hit the road Jack. Just to let you know there a new sheriff in town so I don't need you to pay the bills anymore. You can leave on your own or I can have the police to escort you out." I picked the phone up off the end table and begin to dial 9-1-1.

He didn't say another word. He just grabbed his bags one by one and headed to his car. I was so relieved when he left because I thought I had to put the knife to his ass again. I hate things had to end like this, but he made his bed so now he got to lay in it. After all the bullshit he took me through, I still love him, but I refuse to let him or any man walk over me again. I hope the next bitch treats him like I treated him, but what he needs to realize is that there will never be another me.

Chapter Fifteen
NINO

"OH, MY GOD! What happened to you? Do I need to call the ambulance?" Boo stated all in one breathe as I entered the house. I didn't realize how bad my wounds were until I looked in her full body length mirror that hung behind her front door. Blood was dripping everywhere from the stab wounds, Honeybun really fucked me up.

I looked around the house and noticed it was spic-and-span, just the way I liked it. The aroma of chicken frying tickled my nose and hunger set in.

"No ambulance, I don't want the police in my business. I'll take care of Honeybun myself," I shouted out in anger. "The bitch has lost her damn mind. I told her I didn't want to be with her anymore and she flipped out on me," I lied, with a straight face, while placing my keys on the key hook that hung on the side of me and Boo's photo.

"I told you a long time ago you should've left her, but no, you wanted to continue to mislead the trifling hoe. Making her believe that things were gonna get better between y'all. Now look at you, all cut up. When I see her, I'm gonna tell her about herself."

"No. Leave it alone," I shouted with authority. "I'll handle it myself. She doesn't know about us and I want to keep it that way 'til the time is right."

"When is the time ever gonna be right, Nino? I'm getting tired of this shit. I'm tired of running and hiding our love from the world."

"I don't need to hear yo' nagging right now, Boo. You're preaching to me like a preacher does to his members. All I want you to do is get me a towel to clean my wounds and a towel with ice in it so I can place it on my swollen hand." I yelled out in frustration.

Boo rolled her bubble-eyes at me. I could tell that she was getting aggravated with the fact that I've been living a double life, but she knew I was in a relationship when we started messing around. All Boo wants from me is to come home every night to her and be a one man's woman. Now her wish has come true and I hope our relationship can stand the test of time. In a way, I don't blame Honeybun for her actions. I could have handle things a little better than what I've been doing, but guess what shit happens.

Instead of waiting for Boo to come back with the towels, I headed to the bathroom to take a shower to get the blood off my body. As the water hit my wounds the more pain kicked in. "Ouch," I shouted out in agony. I'm still in shocked behind Honeybun's actions that she took toward me. I never thought she would have enough courage to hit me with a bat, let alone the courage to stab me.

After my shower, Boo and I conversed about our relationship while she patched up my wounds. We talked about what others would think if they found out that we were seeing each other. I must admit, I'm truly in love with her, so what others think at this point doesn't matters. She is the new love of my life and Honeybun just have to deal with it and so does everybody else.

Soon after, Boo brought me a plate filled with fried chicken, macaroni, string beans, garlic bread, a big glass of cold water, and two aspirins. We sat up on the bed and enjoyed dinner together. Immediately after dinner, Boo got on bended knees and took my man hood in her mouth. Her lips being wrapped around my dick made me forget about all the pain that I was in.

$$\$\$\$\$\$\$\$\$\$$

A week has passed since Honeybun beat my ass and I'm healing up faster than I thought. I sat outside the house that I've been paying mortgage on for the last couple of years and noticed that Honeybun haven't left or entered the house. I'm going to put some real heat to her ass whenever I see her. If I knew she was going to flip out on me like this, I would have let Sheena put that bullet in her skull.

Squinting my eyes as I sat on the opposite side of the street from the house, I noticed a for sale sign sticking out the grass. I thought my eyes were deceiving me so I got out the car, slammed the door, and headed in the direction of the for sale sign. *You got to be kidding me,* I spoke to myself. Standing in the grass staring at the sign, I blinked and rubbed my eyes a couple of times as if the sign was going to magically disappear. When I realized that it wasn't, I kicked and jerked on the sign until it was lying in the grass.

"This bitch has lost her fucking mind," I shouted out loud not caring who heard me. "My house is for sale; oh, hell naw. I'm gonna kill this bitch when I get my hands on her." I continued talking loudly to myself. All type of unpleasant things started to pop in my head about Honeybun. What she hasn't realized yet is she just wrote her own death certificate.

Looking over at the mailbox, I noticed there was a pile of mail in it. Seeing all that mail let me know Honeybun haven't been home in a couple of days. Walking swiftly toward the mailbox, I retrieved the mail and sat on the porch. Going through the mail one piece at a time, I came across the light bill, the gas bill, the cable bill, and then I came across an envelope from the bank where Honeybun and I have a joint bank account. Just by looking at the envelope, it didn't look like a bank statement. It looks more so like a business letter.

I opened the letter. As my eyes read from left to right, my hands began to sweat. I can't believe this bitch. She took all the money out my fucking bank account. She's walking around with over $100,000 of my money. Oh yea, this bitch has to be dealt with. I stood up and started to kick on the front door hoping that she would answer. I kicked and kicked and kicked on the door until my foot began to hurt, but there still was no answer. Full of frustrating, I walked off and headed to my car, put my key in the ignition and sped off.

Driving from the suburb to the hood seemed like it was taking forever. I was on a mission to find Honeybun to set her ass straight. I drove around to all the spots where Honeybun normally hang out, but she was nowhere to be found. I picked up my phone and called her trifling friends and they told me they haven't seen her either. I should have known they were going to say that. I continued to drive up and down the streets until I felt myself catching a headache. Thinking about my money Honeybun took and my house being up for sale definitely triggered that headache. As I made a left turn onto Division, I spotted Honeybun and Boo in the gas station having a conversation like they have known each other for years. For a minute, I thought my eyes were deceiving me again, but I can't mistake Boo sexy ass with nobody. I told Boo to stay away from Honeybun and she went against my wishes. I'll deal with her at a later day. Right now, my focus was Honeybun. I parked across the street and watched as the two had a conversation for about five minutes before Honeybun got in her car and pulled off.

Trailing Honeybun had my adrenaline pumping. I trailed her back to the house and parked around the corner. The streets were dark as usual so I wasn't worried about nobody seeing me. I skipped around the block to my house with two dozen of roses in my hands so when I knocked on the door, she wouldn't see my face when she peeped through the peephole. I had the flowers in my car from earlier that day as a surprise for Boo when I made it to her house.

Glancing at the house, I noticed all the lights in the house were still off except for the one upstairs, which was the bedroom light. I stood on the porch for a couple of minutes before ringing the doorbell because I was contemplating if I was going give her a fast or slow death. Honeybun knows that I hate a thief so I don't know why she put herself in this situation. I have a lot of love for her, but she have to go. With flowers in my left hand and my gun in my right hand behind my back, I was ready to show Honeybun that she can't play a nigga like me. After ringing the doorbell three times, I waited patiently for Honeybun to answer.

Chapter Sixteen
Sparkle

Running out of breathe I continued to run down the dark alley. I knew if I stopped at any given moment, my life would be over with. Screaming for help, my cries were not answered. "Help me, somebody help me," I continued to scream as I looked back to see this deranged motherfucker still hot on my heels.

"Sparkle I have no other choice, but to kill you. You know too much."

"I promise I won't tell anybody. It's just between me and you. Please don't kill me." I screamed out while I continued to run. "I'll do anything you want, but please don't take my life."

"I have no choice; you were at the right place, but definitely at the wrong time."

While tears filled up my eyes, my vision began

to become blurry. A gunshot went off and hit me in my right shoulder. My shoulder was burning like a mother-fucker. I continued to run even though I was hit, but tripped and fell over a crate that was in the middle of the alley. With nowhere to go, I just lay there, counted my blessings, and was prepared to go out like a trooper. When J-Boogie stood over me pointing the gun in my face, I could finally put a face to the voice. J-Boogie killed Dee-Man.

Waking up from that nightmare had me sweating. My bed was soaking wet. I sat up in my bed in total shock. As I rocked back and forth in the bed, my hand cradled my mouth because I couldn't believe J was that bald to kill a nigga in front of me. What am I going to do? Just like that, a brilliant idea popped in my head. J-Boogie was getting plenty of money and it's time he share his wealth. He has a choice to either pay me to keep my mouth closed or be prepared to spend the rest of his life in jail. Right now, I'm just going to play it cool to see his reaction when he's around me.

Thinking about Juicy, I knew our friendship was over, but I wasn't going to let it bother me though. Juicy was more so an associate of mine rather than a friend. Despite this being the end of me and her relationship, I really felt sorry for her. Dee-Man must have really pissed J off for him to come into his house to kill him. At this point all I can say is thank God I'm just still alive.

It seemed like my world was falling apart, first I

witness Sheena get killed, then I catch Buttah in the car with Bone, and then my life was almost taken over some dick. It's just been one tragic moment after another, but I'm sure once I come into this money I'm about to blackmail J-Boogie for, I'm going to forget about all the bullshit that have went on.

Finally, building up enough courage to get out of bed, I jumped in the shower to scrub Dee-Man's scent off my body as well as the sweat. After the shower, I lay across my bed contemplating on what I was going to spend all this money on. First, I need to see how much money I was going to ask him for, $50,000 should be enough. Yea I'll ask for $50,000. After I started to think about all the shit I need, $50,000 wasn't nowhere near enough money. Fuck it, I'll ask for $100,000 and move out of town. Nope $100,000 isn't enough either. I know he'll pay more than that for his freedom, $150,000 is what I'll ask for, and I'm not accepting anything less than that. I rolled out of bed, poured myself a glass of wine, and toasted to the money that I was about to come into.

Chapter Seventeen
Buttah

*A*fter a long high speed chase with Derrell we finally lost him. As we passed each block, doing 90mph my heart was beating rapidly. During the whole thing, I prayed that the police didn't get behind us. Going to jail was not an option for me. I had no idea that C-Lo was his cousin. I didn't even know the two knew each other.

After finding an abandon warehouse, we had no other choice but to lay C-Lo to rest. We had too much at stake. Under no circumstances could we keep him alive. Gunz and Marty tied him to a chair. While Gunz had C-Lo's head turned in the opposite direction of the suitcase, the other person held his arm out so I could saw off his wrist.

Screams echoed throughout the abandoned warehouse, but they came to a halt as Gunz put three shots in his head. There was only one way to handle that situation because I didn't want to have to go after Derrell for a code. By Derrell seeing his cousin in the car with me, I knew sooner or later he would be coming to Chicago to looking for some answers.

Lately it seem like every set up is getting messier and messier, but we got to eat so by whatever means we going to get this money. I called J-Boogie and let him know that Derrell might be a problem and he wanted that nigga killed before we left NC, but I talked him out of it. I told him when he come looking for me then we take care of him, until then just let it be.

$$\mathscr{SSSSSSSS}$$

Bone and I have been hitting it off real good, but like the old saying goes 'all good things must come to an end.' I was digging Bone, but not in a relationship type of way. I only wanted to have sex with him one time, but that one time lead to four, five, six more times and still counting. He makes me feel so good when I'm with him. Taking care of me was his specialty. He would run me hot bubble baths and wash each part of my body so soothingly after we finished making love. After I soaked in the tub, he would give me a full body massage, and suck on his popsicles. Popsicles is the nickname he gave my toes. He would suck on them one by one until my body began to quiver. He was just so nice and gentle to me at all times. I wonder was he like that with Sparkle?

The day Bone and I had the car accident with Sparkle we were on our way to the mall on the other side of town. He told me he knew a short cut so we maneuvered through a couple of side streets. I didn't mind being in the car with him because we were way on the other side of town and I wasn't expecting no one to see us together that we knew. I knew if Sparkle found out about me and Bone she was going to go crazy because she was really digging him and it's all because of me he was giving her the cold shoulder.

Once Sparkle ran that stop sign and hit our car, Bone and I sat in the vehicle for a moment trying to gather our thoughts. As I exited the damaged car, I reached down in my Gucci purse to retrieve my mace because I was prepared to spray and beat the driver ass rather it was a woman or man for making me bump my head from the unexpected impact. When I noticed it was Sparkle who hit us, my whole demeanor changed. I was in total shock. The first thing that came to mind was did she do it purposely. I quickly erased that thought out my head because there's no way in the world she could have known that we were going to be on that side of town. Bone and I were the only two who knew where we were going. I was definitely paranoid. I could tell by the look in Sparkle eyes that she was pissed off from seeing me in the car with him. She looked like she wanted to beat my ass, but the bitch better not confused paranoia with being scared. There isn't a scared bone in this body so she better think twice about leaping this way if she knows what's best for her. I know that I'm bogus, but I'm not going to let any bitch beat my ass without a good fight.

Even though I tried speaking to her and clearing things up, she didn't want to hear anything I had to say. I don't want to lose her as a friend, that why first opportunity I get I'm calling things off with Bone. I can't continue to do her this way. Every day I wake up, I regret sleeping with her boyfriends, but it's something about sneaking around with my friend's man that turns me on.

$$\$\$\$\$\$\$\$\$\$$

Visiting hours were from 9am-9pm at Menard Correctional Facility. J-Boogie and I took that seven-hour drive out there to pay Killa a visit. On the way there, we talked about all sorts of things. I just sat in the passenger seat with my seat leaned back, listening attentively.

"Buttah, I think I'm ready to leave this business along and retire." Laughing at my brother as if he had cracked a joke, he cleared his throat and stated. "Stop laughing baby girl, I'm serious. We've been robbing people for a long time. In the beginning, this shit was all fun and games, robbing local boys here and there. Then my pockets got deeper and I needed more money to fill them so I took the show on the road. Nobody was ever supposed to get killed, but I knew there were consequences that came along with hitting boss niggas. K-

Dub raping you really isn't sitting well with me either. I wish I could bring his ass back from the dead and kill him all over again." Still listening attentively, J stated, "Dough-Boy will be our next and last target. Robbing him will set us all straight for life. Oh and by the way, you know I wasn't listening to you about the Derrell situation. He has already been taking care of so you can sleep better at night."

I didn't reply to the Derrell situation. I'm just glad it's over. I also didn't express to J that I was feeling Dough-Boy because I knew he would be upset. I need to try to talk him out of robbing him. If he's broke then he's no good to me, but I knew now was not the time to express how I was really feeling.

"Damn J, I didn't think I would ever hear you say you're ready to get out the game. We've been robbing nigga sense we were teenagers, but I guess your right it's time to give this lifestyle up. I have enough money saved up and I'm sure you do also."

"Yea, baby girl, it's about that time. If them li'l niggas that work with us want to continue to do that shit, that's on them, but me and you are out as soon as we hit Dough-boy."

Pulling into the parking lot of the correctional facility, I stuffed 50 grams of dope in my pussy for Killa. In the letter, he told me not to forget his 50 year old grand-daddy, so I knew exactly what he was talking about. I make sure I bring him that every visit so he can continue to eat. There was money to be made rather he was in the inside or the outside of jail. I wasn't worried about getting caught because he had a couple of female guards he was giving the dick to so they cooperated with no problem.

When Killa walked into the visiting room, his skin had a nature glow to it. His chest and arms were big due to his constant weight lifting. I must admit he was looking good. We greeted each other with a hug and kiss. Killa and J-Boogie gave each other a pound of the fist.

Sitting at the small round table J and Killa got right down to business. "What's good, fam," J spoke aloud.

"I'm glad you came to see me. I got some good news for you. I got some information on a nigga that I know you've been looking to hit."

A wide smile spread across J-Boogie's face. Killa knew all about me, J-Boogie and the crew. "Killa this better be worth my time," J spoke while he continued to smile.

"Believe me it will be. One of the guys in here is from Texas and he told me all about how his guy got down on him that's why he's locked up. He told me dude even ratted out his own momma so he wouldn't have to go to jail and that right there is some grimy shit." At this point, J and I both listen more attentively. I saw the hungry in J-Boogie's eyes. Killa cleared his throat and said, "Guess who his guy is?" Before J had a chance to answer, Killa blurted out, "Dough-Boy."

Hearing Dough-Boy's name was music to his ears, but pain to my heart. What Killa didn't know was Dough boy was next on our hit list. J didn't say anything he just continued to listen.

Killa continued and gave us a full resume on Dough-Boy. He told us where he laid his head, where his baby momma's live, and where his cash houses are. Killa informed us that the setup is definitely going take a lot of planning, which we already knew. He also told us not to rush the job because he is a stone cold killer and he never leaves home without his guns or goons.

From the expression on J-Boogie's face, I knew that the wheels were turning in his head. He knew that it was no room for mistakes. He stated on several occasions he knew the risk with robbing Dough- Boy. He looked at me and stated, "Change of plans. We can't retire just yet. We got to hit a couple more guys while I'm executing a plan to get Dough-Boy."

"Fine by me, nigga. I wasn't ready to retire no way," I stated laughing.

"J-Boogie," Killa stated sternly, "make sure you take care of my angle while she's out there."

"Will do, fam; this my sister. You know I will never let anything happen to her."

"Visiting hours is now over, "the fat white guard yelled. I gave Killa a long kiss and hugged him tightly, longer than usually though. We all parted ways. J and I headed to the express way heading backs to the city.

$$$$$$$$$

Hitting city limits. I got nervous because I was ready to let Bone know that I no longer wanted to carry on our relationship. I can't believe I lost control of the situation. I was only supposed to see how the dick was, get what I can out of him, and be gone. Unfortunately, that didn't happen. For some apparent reason I got hypnotized by his love making. I have to end this immediately because he's taking all my time away from the major players in my life. I really enjoy having sex with him, but he's messing up my flow. I need to move around and so does he. He stopped messing with Sparkle completely according to him on the strength that he wants to be with me, and I don't agree with that at all. I like him, but I don't like him enough to start a relationship with him. I mentioned this to him on several occasions and it seems to goes in one ear and comes out the other. I wasn't trying to take him from her, I just wanted to use him for a couple of hours and send him right back with a smile on his face. Like I told him, he doesn't want to be with me, he just like the way I put it on him. Sparkle told me he wasn't holding any dough, but since he's been with me, I've seen something totally different. He makes sure I have at least $500.00 in my pocket on a daily basis. If it weren't for my girl, I would have considered making him a part of my life. I'm not saying that I was going to make him hubby, but I was definitely going let him join my inner circle. When I deal with niggas, everything is about business. Like the saying goes, "Money over Niggas." I know if I continue to deal with him, he's going to be the biggest problem that I ever encountered in my life. The sooner I break things off with him, the easier it's going to be to get rid of him because he's thinking with the wrong head. It's all Sparkle's fault, though. I know I'm wrong for sleeping with him, but if she weren't running around bragging about how good Bone's dick is, sleeping with him would have never crossed my mind.

Going over to Bone's house, I was a little jittery. I was ready to have the talk with him that we should no longer deal with each other. I drove past his house a couple of times before I went in. Putting my key through the door, I heard him yell out, "Buttah, is that you?"

"Yea, it's me."

"After all this time, I see you finally using your key," he shouted from his bedroom. The purpose of me using the key was in hopes of finding him and another female in the act of things to make the break off simple.

I didn't let him know right away what was on my mind. We watched TV for a while before I decided to bring up the conversation.

"Bone, we need to talk," I said, while laying my head on his chest. I know he was not prepared for what I was about to say, but it needed to be said. I was nervous as hell as he began to rise up, lifting me off his chest. He has become so attached to me; shit, I think he probably loves me.

"What up, my Buttah?" he said, while gazing into my eyes.

I cursed myself for not telling him this over the phone or in an open area so I could run if he wanted to reach out and touch me.

"Baby, I think we need to end our friendship before someone gets hurt."

"What are you talking about? Who's going to get hurt? I love you and you love me." That's what I was afraid of. How could he possible think what he's feeling is love? We have only been seeing each other for some weeks. He's a grown ass man and I can't believe that he doesn't know the difference between love and lust.

"I'm sorry to be so direct, but I don't love you. Sparkle is my friend and we shouldn't be doing this to her."

"Now you wanna have a heart? Hoes don't have a heart. You have never been a friend to her, so why do you want to be a friend now? Friends don't go around sleeping with each other's man."

"What are you talking about?" I shouted, as I eased off the bed and stood with my hands on both my hips.

"Don't act like this is your first time sleeping with one of her men. She told me all about you. You didn't think she knew. She was being the bigger person not to say anything to you, but look what you go and do; you slept with another one of her men. When I saw the way your trifling ass was looking at me, I knew I could have you at any given time, but what I didn't anticipate on doing was falling in love with you. You want to be labeled as classy 'cause you driving around in a Range with your lavish gear and 'cause you own a condo that overlooks Lake Michigan, but truth be told, there's nothing classy about you. You ain't shit, but a five-dollar hoe. The only thing a nigga have to do is show you a couple of dollars and you'll do whateva."

I couldn't believe what I was hearing and the way he was talking to me took me by total surprise. Is this the same guy that I was just with five minutes ago? I was scared out my mind. His attitude changed drastically. I never saw him like this before. I knew that calling things off with him wasn't going to be a smooth transition, but damn, I wasn't expecting a slap in the face either. I couldn't stand there and take his verbal abuse any longer, so I grabbed my belongings, walked out the door, and out of his life.

Chapter Eighteen
BONE

*B*uttah has lost her fucking mind thinking it was going to be easy to leave me. Leaving me is not an option. I'm in love with her, even though she's a gold digging ass bitch. I know with my guidance she can be the perfect woman. I'm the only man she needs in her life. She already said she never had a man to lay the pipe down like me. She thought she was going to fuck me good, use me for my money, and then leave me. She got the game all screwed up. I wear the fucking pants, not her. Either she's going to be with me, or Sparkle will find out about us without a doubt and that's not a threat it's a promise.

It took all I had in me not to knock her off her feet when she told me she didn't want to be with me anymore. Playing with my feelings is like playing with fire. If you fuck me over, prepare to be burned. I'm not going to deny that ever since I saw Buttah, I've been infatuated by her beauty and the way she carries herself. When I first laid eyes on her, all the blood in my body rushed to my woman pleaser. It was something about that girl that turned me on, and I needed her in my life without a doubt.

When I first met Sparkle, I felt the same way about her. Her beauty was so unique. Her skin had a special glow to it, and her ass was so perfect and round. I nicknamed her "Apple Bottom." I knew something wasn't right about her though, but I just couldn't put a finger on it until I seen her in traffic giving a nigga some head.

I was leaving the club one night and was caught at a red light on Madison and Pulaski. When I glanced over to the left of me, I saw a nigga getting some head. I wasn't trying to be nosey, I was just being aware of my surroundings. All I seen was the back of the chick head and her back. Her shirt was a belly top so I had a good view of the lower part of her back. When I saw the trap stamp that read "Sparkle," hurt and anger overtook me at the same time. Like I said before I knew something wasn't right with her, I just didn't know if it was good or bad. She led me to believe that I was the only one. This is why I never exposed to her the real me and never was able to make her my woman. There are a lot of things she doesn't know about me. I only allow people to hear and see what I want them to hear and see when it comes to me.

$$$$$$$$

"Nigga, what you doing tonight?" I asked my brother over the phone because we haven't kicked it in a while and I needed a drink to take my mind off Buttah.

"Nothing much, I didn't have anything planned besides getting money."

"How about we meet up tonight at that new strip club they just opened on Weed Street."

"Oh that sounds like a plan. Ray-Ray and some other guys went there last weekend and they said that place is better than Strip Tease. What time should I be there?"

"Be there around 10:00."

"All right, see you there."

The ladies in the building were immaculate. There wasn't a stripper insight over 25. Yep, this definitely was my type of strip club. I hated going to strip clubs where they had old bitches that were older than my mom stripping. I loved looking at young perky breasts not saggy breast.

I sat in VIP, waiting for my brother to arrive. In the meantime, I enjoyed my lap dance and my drinks. I order me two Blue Motherfuckers to hold me until my brother arrived. The night was still young so I knew we were going to be there for a while.

"Yo, Marcus," I yelled out, when I spotted him. Yelling out didn't get his attention. What was I thinking? He wasn't going to be able to hear me over the loud music. I told the stripper I'll be right back and not to move.

I tapped Marcus on his shoulder and gave him a brotherly hug then we headed back to V.I.P. "Bro, Ray-Ray didn't lie when he told me this place is better than Strip tease." Marcus stated to me while he pulled out his dollars getting ready for a night full of fun.

We sat in VIP, enjoying our lap dances and talking shit. Since Marcus arrived, I ordered a bottle of Remy and a bottle of Moet. Every time my brother drinks, his mouth runs a hundred words a minute. He started talking about this chick that he wanted to wife.

"I got this bad bitch on my team bro. The bitch so bad she makes you wanna kiss her momma." I couldn't do shit but laugh. He thinks he's a comedian at times.

"Bro, that bitch that bad? I need to meet her. Does she have any friends or sisters?"

"Naaaaw, man, she don't have any sisters, but she have plenty of friends and all of 'em are sexy as hell. She a cool girl and I'm digging her, but there are a lot of things that she has to change about herself before I make her my woman. She's a smart dummy. She thinks money is everything and I can't have a gold digger as my woman. Any female I wife needs to have a goal. The only goal she has is to see how many pockets she can get in during the course of the day. She has a lot of potential, but she has a lot of growing up to do also.

I'm trying to steer her in the right directions, but I can only do so much without spelling it out. I'm not gonna front, her head game is good as hell and what's between her legs should be illegal. That's why I gotta wife her, dawg."

"Yo, if you feel like that, keep her on yo' team. Just be patient with her. She might come to her senses sooner than you think," I stated after taking a sip on my drink, "but if she doesn't, treat her like the hoe she is and keep it moving. Don't be blinded by the pussy or the head. Pussy that lethal shouldn't be played with. Keep that in mind, but like you said, maybe with a little guidance, she can be the one. By the way, what's her name? I might have slept with her a couple of times since you say she like niggas with deep pockets." I responded jokingly. I was only joking about sleeping with her not the deep pockets.

"Sparkle is the chick name."

My right eyebrow quickly rose up, "did you say the chick name is Sparkle. What she look like?"

"Why? Do you know her or something?"

"Maybe. I don't know. Just describe the hoe."

When I asked him what the girl name was, I wasn't expecting him to say Sparkle. I still had sexual feelings for her despite me catching her with a dick in her mouth and despite me being in love with her friend. I still planned on fucking her from time to time. When he described her phat ass, her round beautiful face, her thick thighs, and her tramp stamp, I knew it was the same person. This hoe just keep going and going like the energizer bunny. Its official she's nothing, but a two dollar hoe. First, I caught her in the car and now, I find out she's sleeping with my brother. I guess it ain't no fun if yo' homey can't have none. In my case, brother. I guess me and my brother share more than genes. I told my brother we both were fucking the same hoe. He had a quizzical look on his face. I knew that he was upset, but he couldn't show it. The rule was no hoes before blood.

He sucked it up like a man and replied, "Maybe we can have her at the same time," while guzzling down a glass of Moet. I'm sure any thought he had about making her his wife, had just went straight out the window.

I didn't let that ruin my night. We popped another bottle of Moet to help us take our minds off that hoe Sparkle and to ease our minds of the daily pressure we go through to survive in these vicious streets.

The strip club was still popping. The more niggas arrived the more strippers came out. They were walking around with nothing on, but a G-string. Titties were bouncing everywhere, from small, medium, to large, and asses were jiggling like JELLO. This one particular stripper, named Pineapple dropped it like it's hot when she hit the stage. Her theme song was *She Got a Donk* by Soulja Boy. The attire that she wore was nothing, but a G-string and stars to cover her pink perky nipples. She was the thickest white female I ever seen in my life. She didn't have any cellulite on her body, like most thick chicks do. She must work out on a daily basis. She did all type of tricks with that pussy to get them hundreds out my hands. She worked the pole like she was a firefighter. I was intrigued with the way she swung around that pole, hair swinging from side to side, while her titties bounced up and down. She blew my mind when she blew a whistle with her pussy. That was one bad white chick.

Once she finished dancing, she strolled over to where I was, with nothing on, bent over toward me, licked my ear, and whispered, "Thanks for the generous tip. I want to do something special for you." I didn't hesitate to tell her to do what was on her mind. She reached toward my private area, pulled my long chocolate stick out, massaged it until it became rock hard, and slid a strawberry flavored condom on with her mouth. The chick definitely had my undivided attention. She proceeded and sucked my dick until she gagged a couple of times getting her mouth as moist as it could get. Afterward, she rode my dick backward and ass facing me, as if it was the last dick on earth. Club X-Rated will definitely get more of my business because anything goes. That club is a big ass orgy. Niggas was fucking to the left and to the right of me. This was definitely the place to be on the weekend.

Passing out hundreds of dollars to Pineapple that night wasn't anything. I wipe my ass with money. I could own her ass if I wanted to, that's just how much money I got. A lot of females think I don't have it like the next man, but truth be told, I have it better than the next man. I am the man. I'm very discreet at what I do. I supply the whole Westside with them white bricks. I don't need attention because all attention ain't good attention, that why I left Atlanta and moved to Chicago. I came here with a whole new agenda.

After my sexual escapade with Pineapple, Marcus and I stayed at the club for about 30 more minutes and then bounced. We jumped into his Cadillac truck and drove off with the wind, leaving my car parked at the club.

"Big bro, I want to show you something." He stated intoxicated.

"Go right ahead." He passed me a fat ass swisha filled with 'dro and told me to light it while he popped in a DVD. Marcus had his truck dressed up nicely. His truck was black-on-black, sitting on 24-inch rims. The front grill and handles on each door were chromed out also, and every headrest had its own TV. He also had a nice sound system that made his windows shake every time bass came blasting through the speakers. I hit the blunt four times then passed it to the left of me. When the movie started, I choked and my eyes damn near popped out my head because of what I was seeing. On the homemade flick, Sparkle was sucking Marcus' dick like a professional. She sucked his dick and juggled his balls in her mouth until all his babies dropped down her throat. Moments later, Buttah walked into the room.

She rubbed Sparkle's body, laid her on her back, and gave her what looks like some mind-blowing head. After seeing the movie, I had no respect for her or Sparkle. I watched the movie in its entirety. Damn, Buttah had me fooled also. I knew she wasn't an angel, but I wasn't expecting her to be a carpet-muncher. Of course, Marcus jointed in their sexual act. They were fucking like there was no tomorrow. I was heated sitting there watching the flick. I guess if you flaunt the money bitches are willing to do whatever.

After watching the flick it took all I had in me that night not to jump in my car and drive to Buttah house and kick her in her pussy. I had so many different emotions going through me. If it weren't for me seeing the flick, I would still be trying to make Buttah my woman. I thought she was the one. Just a couple of days ago I went ring shopping for her. I'm glad I didn't make the mistake of purchasing it. I guess if I want a good woman I got to go the suburbs or to church.

Chapter Nineteen

Nino

"Who is it," I heard Honeybun shout through the door. I didn't say a word. I remained quiet as a smile came across my face behind the roses from the anticipating of me killing her. Still waiting patiently on the front porch my trigger finger was ready to send her to be in the presence of the Lord. 'Who is it," she shouted again and of course I didn't say a word. I heard her playing with the lock on the door, but the door never opened. "Kane is that you." I heard her say." *Kane, who the fuck is Kane? I can't believe she got a nigga coming to my house.* "Bae, those roses are beautiful," she said, as she peeped through the peephole. "The door is jammed again just give me a minute."

As she continued to jerk and twist on the door knob, the door wouldn't open so she instructed me to use the back door. Running to the back of the house, I tripped over a garbage can, but bounced back on my feet quickly.

By the time I got to the back of the house, the door was wide open. I checked my surrounding to make sure she wasn't on any bullshit. Right after she heard the door slam she yelled, "I'm up stairs."

Placing the flowers on the kitchen counter, I headed upstairs to give Honeybun what she deserved. She's really going to regret taking my shit. The lights were cut down low and soft music was playing when I reached the room. Her naked body was spread across the bed. I couldn't believe she was ready to fuck another nigga in my bed. I wasn't ready to take her out of her misery just yet. I want some pussy for the last time so I tossed the gun on a chair that was in the room.

"Hey, there, daddy's home."

"What the fuck you doing in my house, Nino," she screamed out, as she scrambled to throw the cover over her body.

"I told you before, Honeybun, this is my damn house and I can come and go as I please. I see you got that pussy nice and wet for daddy," I stated, as I begin to unbuckle my pants.

"Nino, I'm not your woman anymore. This pussy does not belong to you."

"Let me guess, it belongs to that nigga, Kane, who you thought was at the door."

"I don't want any trouble, Nino. Can you please just leave?"

"Leave? I'm not going anywhere until I get some pussy. Give me some pussy and I'll leave," I stated, as I continued to unbuckle my pants.

I noticed her contemplating on what she wanted to do, but she gave in without a fight. "See, that's my girl," I stated, as I entered her.

After having rough sex with Honeybun, I knew I had to complete what I came over there to do. If I didn't take care of her, she would think she could get away with fucking me over and I couldn't let that happen.

"Still lying in the bed, I spoke calmly, "So you thought you were just going to rob a nigga blind huh?"

I knew I caught her off guard, and she replied, "What are you talking about Nino."

"Honeybun, we can make this easy or we can make this hard. Take your pick. Where is my damn money?"

Once again, she gave me an answer that I didn't want to hear. Placing my hand around her neck, I choked the bitch until tears begin to walk down her face.

"Heidi, I'm not going to keep asking you the same question. Where the fuck is my money?" I loosen the grip around her neck giving her a chance to answer, but she didn't. "Okay, so this is how you want to play it. Fine by me."

I tossed her on the floor, and gave her a few good stumps. I pointed my dick in the direction of her face and gave her a nice golden shower. I was through asking her questions. I knew she wasn't going to give me my money back. I can just chop that up as a loss. After her golden shower, I grabbed the gun off the chair and emptied the gun of all the bullets except one.

"Let's play a little game of rush and roulette. Bitch, I'm gonna give you the pleasure of killing yourself."

"No, Nino, No. Okay, okay. I'll give you your money back, but I can't get a hold of it until tomorrow."

"Stop lying; give me my fucking money now. I stated as I twirled the chamber of the gun."

"Okay Nino, let me get up. It's in the closet."

I stepped to the side and let Honeybun get up off the floor. I knew regardless if I got my money back or not, I still was going to kill her. I really do have love for Honeybun, but she double crossed me and there is no way I can look over that.

"You bitch ass nigga," was all I heard as Honeybun aimed her very first Christmas present at me. I forgot all about that damn gun. Not ever having a chance to react all I could do was run my naked ass out the house.

Jumping in my car I reached in my back seat and grabbed me one of my outfits that I never gotten a chance to drop off at the cleaners. Honeybun has really loss her damn mind I spoke loudly as I hit the steering wheel of my car. No more playing game with this crazy bitch. Next time I see her I'm just going to shoot her

point blank. There will be no more talking. I jumped on
I-88 and headed straight to Boo's house to check her
ass for talking to Honeybun. Bitches just don't listen
these days.

"Get your ass up," I yelled as Boo slept peaceful-
ly on the couch.

"Why are you yelling? What's wrong baby?"

"Don't play stupid with me. Yo' ass don't listen. I
told you to stay away from Honeybun and don't say you
wasn't talking to her earlier today because I saw it with
my own two fucking eyes."

"It's not what you think Nino."

"Boo stop fucking playing with me before I beat
your ass."

"Nino, let me tell you something. I'm not Honeybun. I don't take to well to threats and I definitely
don't take ass beating. Now calm you ass down so I can
explain."

"Okay Boo explain," I stated in a much calmer
voice as I rubbed my hands over hers that was almost
the same size as my hands.

"Bae, as I was leaving out the gas station playing
my lottery. I saw her pulling in. I tried my best to hurry
to my car and pull off because I really wanted to tell her
about herself, but I remember what you said. As I was
getting in my car, she walked up to my car and asked
me a question about my rims. So, I got out the car and I
guess this is the part when you saw us talking and I told
her where she could go get the rims at and that was it. I

went my way and she went her way."

"Are you sure that's all y'all talked about, Boo?

"Yes baby I'm sure. I will never go against your words. I love you too much."

"I'm sorry baby for coming in here snapping. I've had one hell of a day."

"Do you want to talk about it?"

"Naw, baby, I rather not." I reached out toward Boo's face, brought it close to mine, and gave her a long passionate tongue kiss. "I love you, baby."

"I love you, too."

$$\$\$\$\$\$\$\$\$\$$

The next morning I headed to my block to check on my workers. I stopped at Clara's, which is a mom-and-pop restaurant that set on the same street my joint was on. I took a window seat in the restaurant to observe my workers. Those little niggas have been slipping lately. *I might have to make an example out of one of them if they don't get their priorities straight,* I thought to myself as I sat, enjoying my turkey bacon, scrambled eggs with cheese and cheese grits. Staring out the window, I seen a clean ass sky blue Cutlass, sitting on 28inch rims. The car looked like my car except my car was maroon. My worker severed him what look like from where I was sitting a couple of bags of weed. My eyes followed as he pulled off and my eyes landed on his license plates. I ran out of the restaurant screaming to my workers catch that car, but it was too late.

The car had pulled over, leaving us to linger in his dust.

Jumping in my car, I yelled for Twon to jump in the car with me. He did, without any questions.

"Reach in my glove compartment, li'l nigga, and give me some bullets."

"Who we got to kill, boss man?" Twon asked, as he took his gun off safety.

"That dude you just served in that Cutlass is driving my car."

"I thought your Cutlass was maroon? And how in the hell did he get your car without your permission."

"I got a good idea of how he got it and that bitch will be taking care of real soon. Have you seen dude that's driving the car around here before."

"Naw, boss man. That was some white dude driving that car. At first, I wasn't going to serve him 'cause I thought he was the police."

Pulling in the gas station behind the car, I got out my vehicle and startled dude when I knocked on my window with the gun causing him to drop his weed out his blunt.

"Let the window down, homie. I got some questions for you"

Scared out his mind, he let the window down, "What can I help you with?"

"First thing first, put you damn hands down. I'm not here to rob you."

"Okay," he stated, nervously.

"Where did you get this car from?"

"I bought it from some chick name Heidi that was advertising it in the newspapers."

That was all the confirmation that I needed. After he told me what I wanted to hear, I let him go about his merry way. My beef was with Honeybun, not him.

Chapter Twenty
BUTTAH

I woke up this morning feeling nauseous. I ran from my bedroom toward the bathroom and buried my face into my porcelain toilet. I couldn't believe I was regurgitating again. Everything I ate the previous night was now in the toilet. This has been going on for about a week now and I'm ready to come to reality with myself that I might be pregnant by Bone, but I'm still praying it's the stomach flu. I placed both my hands underneath the cold water that was running in the sink and splashed it onto my face. I glanced at the mirror in front of me and noticed I looked terrible. Sixty seconds later, my eyes watered, and I found myself bending over regurgitating again. The fear of me being pregnant by Bone outweighed the thought of me having the stomach flu. *This can't be happening,* I thought to myself. I know this fool didn't knock me up. I can't have his baby. Having his baby will only slow me down, and besides I'm not ready for that type of responsibility. On top of that, what will I tell Sparkle.

Once I stopped vomiting I jumped in my Range and drove to the drug store down the street from where I lived to get a pregnancy test. I wasn't feeling or looking sexy at all. I had on my Juicy Couture jogging suit, a baseball cap, and a pair of all white air-max, something that I rarely wore. I drove around the parking lot a couple of times before I found a parking space. I jumped out my truck and right before I got to the entrance I threw up again. Luckily, I had a bottle of water in my hand to wash away the nasty taste I just encountered. The only thought that kept coming to my mind was what if the test comes back positive, and if it does, I'm calling the first abortion clinic I see in the yellow pages.

I can't believe I allowed myself to get caught like this. I regret ever sleeping with him. Most females get pregnant on purpose, thinking they can trap a man, but in my situation, the roles were reversed. Out of all the women he slept with, why I had to be the one to get pregnant. I'll be the first to admit to any man that I ain't shit. I did the relationship thing before and being single feels much better. I can't be nobody's mother, not now anyway. He knows that I slept with Sparkle's previous boyfriends, so why would he want me to begin with. It's something else going on between him and Sparkle that he's not telling me and I'm determined to find out.

I entered the drugstore and asked the young freckle-faced clerk standing at register one to point me in the direction of the pregnancy tests so I wouldn't be walking around the whole store looking confused. He directed me to aisle four. While picking up the test, I bumped into one of my enemies from high school. Out of all the people I could have seen that day, why did it have to be her? I hated her with a passion and she hated me with the same passion if not more.

Tasha looked me up and down with a frown on her face and I returned the same look. She had animosity toward me because I stole her boyfriend when we were in high school. Well, I really didn't steal him, he just chose me over her.

It was the fall of '02 when I transferred to the high school. It was my sophomore year and they were juniors. By me being the new girl at the school with the pretty face and banging body, all the guys were attracted to me, especially her boyfriend TJ.

TJ was this six foot five inch shooting guard with huge feet. *You know what they say about boys with big feet.* TJ was a very attractive young man. I never really cared about his looks or any others guy's looks. It was all about what they had in their pockets that determined if they would get the time of day, but for some apparent reason I was drawn to his masculine beauty. His skin was the perfect shade of brown. He didn't have a single scar on his face as most men had; his skin was flawless. His body was cut up so perfectly that he would put the average man to shame. He wore his hair just like the singer Omarion, but his braids were a little shorter. Every day after my lunch period, he would be standing by my locker waiting for me with a rose in his hand. Tasha caught him after the third time and they got into a massive altercation. They both were suspended for three days. When they returned to school, he was still trying to get with me. After several attempts, with his persuasive and charming personality, I gave in. We started dating and Tasha was history. If he hadn't been killed in a car accident five months after we started dating, I really do believe that we would still be together. Killa, nor any other man, would have ever gotten a chance. After his accident, I was devastated. I lost control of myself and started sleeping with everybody. I was looking for love in all the wrong places.

My trip down memory lane was interrupted when I saw Dough-Boy walking down the aisle calling her name looking like Denzel Washington in his younger days. I hope this is his sister or cousin, but in the back of my mind, I knew this was a bitch he was seeing. I can't imagine her being his main female, but if so she making it much easier for me to get him because she's definitely no competition. As he walked down the aisle past the tampons, I gave him a sexual stare. He noticed and smiled slightly at me. Tasha noticed our eye contact and looked at me and said, "Don't get fucked up." I just looked at her and smiled. Being the bold bitch that I am, I yelled out my number and told him, "If you want a real woman on your arm, holla at ya girl." I walked off giggling and headed to the register to check out.

Walking through the sliding door, Tasha ran up on me totally catching me off guard. She was a little heavier and taller than me, so when she pushed me I went flying to the ground. She ran toward me trying to kick me, but I was too quick for her. I bounced to my feet and knocked the shit out of her with my right fist. She went flying into a parked minivan. Once she bounced back to her feet, we went toe to toe. I stole on her and she stole back. Somehow, in the middle of our catfight, I sprung my ankle and fell to the ground and she started to kick the shit out of me. She kicked me in the head, back, and stomach while I screamed out in pain. Dough-Boy finally made it outside the store and stopped the fight and all I could say to myself was "about time." He grabbed her by the arm and told her to get in the car. She didn't obey and stayed right where she was. She started waving her hands from side to side and words were coming out her mouth like diarrhea until he smacked her in it. Immediately after that, she went running to the car.

"Are you all right," he asked; as he bent down to help me from the ground.

Embarrassed, I responded, "Never felt better," but gigging in between each word. "But seriously, my ankle is in pain and my stomach is cramping." At that very moment, all I could think about was my unborn child. Even though I didn't want the baby, I didn't want my enemy to kill it. If I lose my baby, I'm going to make her life a living hell.

"Dough-Boy, forget her. Leave that bitch where she's at. Let's go." Tasha yelled from his car. Hearing the aggravation in her voice was music to my ears.

"Tasha, I don't have time for your bullshit. Just sit there and shut up."

"What you mean shut up? I'm your woman not her! You supposed to be over here assisting me."

Dough-Boy didn't say anything else to her or look her way. All his attention was focused on helping me to my car and making sure I was all right. I was enjoying every moment.

$$\mathscr{SSSSSSSS}$$

Back at my apartment, I immediately pissed on the white stick and waited patiently for it to reveal one or two lines. I was nervous as hell. Those three minutes I waited for the results seemed like three hours. I was too nervous to look at the test so I took a hot Epsom salt bath to relieve my ankle from the aching pain.

Before exiting the bathroom, reality smacked me in my face. I was indeed pregnant. At that moment the only question that popped in my mind was should I tell Bone's crazy ass. In a way, I felt he was entitled to know because he was the father, but on the other hand, I was like fuck him. I quickly dismissed the idea of letting him know because if he knew it would only complicate our situation more.

Having a baby was not in my plans. I can't be tied down with a child because of my current lifestyle. Once I get a couple of millions in my bank account and travel to every city in North America, I might consider starting a family, but until then I'm going to live my life childless.

I lay in my bed with my foot propped up on two pillows to alleviate some of the pain that I was still feeling. I quickly grabbed my phone from my night stand so I could call my girls. I told them all about the fight I had with Tasha. I also told them to meet me at my crib in an hour so we can talk business because there was money to be made.

Honeybun was the first to arrive. She walked in with a big smile on her face. Something was different about her, was it her hair, shoes, or outfit? I just couldn't pinpoint it. She was definitely glowing. Could she be pregnant? I hope not because Nino would definitely try to run her life and dictate her every move.

I couldn't take the suspense anymore so I asked, "Why are you so damn happy?"

"So you noticed. I'm glad you asked. I finally put Nino ass out the house and I beat his ass with my bat and stab the nigga. Then the fool had the nerve to show back up the other day and I had to shoot at his sorry ass"

"You've gotta be kiddin' me!"

"Why would I do a thing like that? Girl, it was

time I set that nigga free. I've been with him for too long for him not to appreciate me. I was his back bone and his shoulder to lean on, but he never realized it. I was tired of sitting in the house being a fool while he was out having a good time with God knows who. I just couldn't take another night waking up without my man lying next to me. I felt as long as he had the title of being my man, he had to live by the house rules or be gone."

"What took ya so long? You should have been putting that bat upside his head. Every morning he put his key in the door I would have been standing on the other side greeting him with that bat in hand. I still can't believe you finally stood up to him," I laughed. "He deserved everything you gave him. Niggas always fuck up with the good ones."

"I'm glad he fucked up 'cause I have a new man that treats me with respect."

"Giiiiiirl, I can't believe you got a new man already. Damn, you move fast. You need to slow down before you find yourself in the same situation you were just in. I'm not trying to throw salt in your game, but be careful. I wish you the best."

Right before Honeybun could elaborate on her next sentence, my house phone began to ring. It was the front desk clerk letting me know that I had another guest. About a week prior, a young lady was stabbed to death by her baby's daddy. She had a restraining order on him because he used to beat her ass on a daily basis.

The crazy fool stabbed her thirty-seven times, and then he jumped out the window and killed himself. I never understood why men beat women when they are supposed to cherish us. Ever since then, the building manager came up with a new security measure to protect the tenants. Every guest that visit have to past a criminal background check to get in the building, they had to sign in and out, call up to the apartment to announce their arrival, and give the front desk a four digit password that was assigned to each tenant. If the background check was in progress at the time, there was no way old girl's baby's daddy would have gotten a chance to get in the building.

I told Honeybun to unlock the front door and I ran straight to the bar and poured myself two shots of Hennessy. I gulped the shots down feeling the burning sensation in my chest. I wasn't really prepared to be in Sparkle's presence sober knowing I was pregnant by her ex-man.

"Hey," Sparkle said as she entered my living room, looking like she just got off somebody's runway. She was dressed in this one-shouldered Dolce & Gabbana dress that hugged every curve of her body, a matching jeweled clutch, and a pair of "come fuck me" pumps. I must give it to her, the girl was looking fuckable. If Honeybun wasn't there, I would have went in my room and got one of my strap-ons, the 12-inch one, and gave it to her like I was a nigga. I know for a fact that she wanted me because she's always asking me to join in on a threesome with her. I know if I lick it one more good time, she would forget about ever seeing me and Bone together.

"What's good girly?" Honeybun spoke, then me.

"You tell me what's good, Buttah? You are the one who invited me over here," she state with a semi attitude directed toward me.

I wasn't about to let this bitch get under my skin. I invited them over for one reason and one reason only and that's to discuss money. If she was in, it's all good, but if not more money for me and Honeybun because I know my girl was down for whatever since she wasn't with Nino anymore.

"Well, the purpose of inviting you chicks over here is to discuss money. I know you both love money as much as I love it. I basically live for them dead presidents. You both know what I do for a living, which is set niggas up. Me and my brother have been discussing adding more females to the business. I can't do this by myself and what other females would I choose besides my bottom bitches to help orchestrate our business. Honeybun, you know how we get down 'cause you used to be a part of the team."

"Wait a minute," Sparkle stated cutting me off. "You set niggas up. I never knew you did that shit. I just thought you fucked and sucked for a couple of bucks. This shit you talking is risky. This is some shady shit you doing. If these niggas find out what we doing they will kill us. I'm down for the mighty dollar too, but not this way."

"I understand your concern, but these guys out here are so green. They want even see us coming, but if they do figure it out we would be so far gone they will never catch us. We wouldn't be setting niggas up here in Chicago; we would be flying state to state where no one knows us. That's where I be when I tell you I'm out on a business trip for my brother. This shit we doing is fool proof. Do you think my brother would put me in danger? He scope out every nigga before he send me on a job. I'm not trying to put any pressure on you, but if you want to make some real money, I'm willing to help you out. Fucking and sucking on dicks ain't gonna get you the lifestyle I'm living, honey."

"Yea, she's right Sparkle. This shit is like stealing candy from a kid. If I wouldn't have gotten involved with Nino, I know for a fact I would still be doing this shit with my girl. Believe me when I say it, it's worth the money. Half of the time, you don't have to lay on your back. Just drug the nigga up, make the phone call and when he wake up everything he ever owned is gone."

"It sounds good, but let me think on it."

"There's nothing to think about. Let's get this money and stop playing girl. Buttah, you already know I'm in." Honeybun said excitedly, sounding like a woman who just received her income tax check.

"There no rush Sparkle, take your time, but the longer you wait the more money you missing out on. As a matter of fact, in three days, I'm flying out to do two jobs. Honeybun, you can have one and Sparkle; you come with me so I can show you how easy this shit is. Just keep in mind; these niggas don't know us from a can of paint. They think new pussy is good pussy."

Even though Sparkle was second guessing joining the team, I continued to talk to her until she finally gave in. I finally brought up the subject of me having the fight with Tasha and how my Superman Dough-Boy came to the rescue. We all agreed that we were going to deal with Tasha later, but our main focus at the time was getting this money.

Chapter Twenty-One
SPARKLE

*A*in't this some shit? As soon as I stepped off the plane in Atlanta, it was pouring. I could have stayed in Chicago if I wanted to put up with unpredictable weather. The whole plane ride to Atlanta, there was silence between me and Buttah. She knows as well as I know she fucked Bone. That's why she wants to put me onto her and J-Boogie's hustle. Her conscience is eating at her.

Walking through the airport, I broke the silence, "So what's next?"

"We head to the hotel, freshen up, and have fun until we receive further instructions from J-Boogie."

"What instructions are we waiting for?" I asked with a nonchalant attitude. I was trying my best to keep my composure and be civilized, but I just have so much anger built up inside of me when it came to her. At that moment, I could have given her a nice beat down to remember, and maybe, just maybe, she wouldn't sleep with another one of my men.

"Basically, who and when we will be setting the nigga up. Girl, I told you there is nothing to be afraid of. Just go with the flow and keep in mind that it's a job, so be professional at all times."

Instantly, I snapped. "Bitch, what you mean be professional at all times?" *Was this bitch trying to insinuate that I'm ghetto?*

"Like I said, be professional at all times. I'm not trying at come at ya the wrong way, but these niggas we setting up have lots of money. If they sense an ounce of ghetto in you, they not gonna look your way." I know she saw the hatred in my eyes, but she continued, "These niggas are loaded with cash that we rob. It has been plenty of times I wanted to cuff one of the money makers, make 'em my man, but went with my better judgment. All I'm saying is do not, I mean, under any circumstances, fall in love with the nigga because you will put yourself in harm's way."

Before I could respond to what she was saying, her cell phone rang, interrupting my next response. At that very moment all I could think about was the type of money I would and could be making if I took on a couple of jobs. I wasn't looking to do this permanently. I just want to make a couple of thousands and get out. Maybe then I can own a Range and live in a condo downtown. Don't get me wrong, I'm comfortable with my lifestyle and where I'm living, but there is always room for improvement.

Once off the phone, she broke everything down to me. We talked about the good and the bad parts of the business. The part that I hated most...fuck, there was no part. I hated everything about setting the niggas up because karma is a motherfucka. Honestly, having sex with these niggas didn't bother me one bit. I love trying new things, if you know what I mean. There's nothing better than an even trade; sex for money. She also mentioned that tomorrow we would be making our move. They got word that Lucky, the guy we were setting up, would be at this Annual Playa's Ball. I was excited because I always wanted to go to the Playa's Ball here in Atlanta.

$$$$$$$$$

Waking up the next evening, I was nervous and exciting at the same time. I didn't want anything to go wrong so I woke Buttah up and asked her to go over the instructions again. She explained with no problem.

The day was flying by so fast and the night was quickly approaching. We didn't do much that day beside eat, drink, and talked some more about the business. I wanted to have things down packed before I went out on this job.

After speaking with Buttah and taking a long hot shower at the hotel, I began to loosen up a bit and my whole demeanor about setting these guys up changed drastically. Buttah and Honeybun did make valid points back in Chicago. At that moment, I began to relax a little more, and I even started to let my mind ease off the fact that I saw Bone and her together. One of my ex-boyfriends told me, "A hoe will be a hoe no matter how you try to change her 'cause it's in her blood. Friend or no friend, you just got to let a hoe do her job," and I totally agree.

Choosing my outfit for the night took some time. I had to choose wisely. I wasn't lacking in the looks or body department by far, but I didn't want to come off as a slut, or make it obvious that I was there to seduce someone. When I walked through the door I wanted my outfit to send a signal out to every man that if you like what you see now, wait until you take off my clothes, but my signal was directed toward one individual, which was Lucky.

Walking into the Playa's Ball all eyes were on me. There were pimps and hoes everywhere, and of course, you had your wannabe's in attendance. I was dressed in a Gucci opened back short jump suit, with the matching hand bag, and matching four inch pumps. Ass was just jiggling everywhere. Buttah and I decided that we would arrive at the ball at different times only because if I didn't grab Lucky's attention, then she would. One of us was definitely going to get him.

I walked around for several minutes before I spotted my target in the corner by the bar with his fan club. I knew I had to work extra hard to get his attention because women were everywhere. I noticed he was buying drinks for all the ladies around him so I pranced over to where they were to blend in with the crowd. I mingled with the crowd for about twenty minutes before I noticed Buttah making her entrance and boy was she dressed for the event. She was dressed in this sequined, mini Miu Miu dress that made her legs look long and slender. She had her hair pulled back into a bun, showing off her beautiful facial features, making her very pleasing to the eye. She kept her distance while I tried to work my number. I stayed with the crowd working my way closer to Lucky. When I got close enough, I leaned on the bar, flagged down the bartender, and ordered me a drink.

"Let me get that for you Lil Momma," Lucky stated when he saw me reaching in my purse to get my money.

"No, I got it."

"But I insist. I'll be less of a man if I let a woman as beautiful as you pay for her own drink." He stated screaming over the loud music, while walking closer to me and rubbing his hands over his neatly trimmed beard.

I extended my hand to meet his, "I'm Sparkle, and you are?"

"Nice to meet you Sparkle, I'm Lucky."

"Nice to meet you also, for some particular reason I feel like it's my lucky night, Mr. Lucky."

"Why would you say that, beautiful lady?"

"Only because it's about a hundred different women in here all shapes, shades, and sizes and you're over here entertaining me."

"Well, I guess you can consider yourself the lucky one. Are you from Atlanta?"

"As a matter of fact I am, born and raised." I lied right through my teeth with a straight face.

"Oh okay, well I just moved here about five years ago. My job offered me a better position with higher pay so I jumped on that band wagon with no questions asked."

Better paying position I can agree with, but job, tell that shit to somebody that don't know any better. I thought briskly to myself. We continued to talk with each other over the loud music. The DJ was getting down on the ones and twos. People was partying like it was 1999, Prince couldn't have said it any better. Moments later, Buttah walked over to where we were. I noticed that he was instantly attracted to her as soon as he laid his pretty, gray, bedroom eyes in her direction. She walked up positioning herself on the other side of him. She ordered herself a drink and walked away without saying a word. I know he wanted to say something to her and offer to buy her drink, but he didn't out of respect for me. His eyes followed her until she was out of his view.

I broke the silence between us. "So you like what you see," totally catching him off guard. He didn't respond he just smiled. "She was beautiful." I spoke loudly to let him know exactly what and who I was referring to.

"Yes, indeed she was."

Quickly getting right to the point, "What you doing' after you get out of here."

"Nothing in particular, do you have something in mind," he asked.

"Yep, as a matter of fact I do. Maybe we can get out of here and go to a quieter place so we can get to know each other better," I stated, flirtatiously while twirling my hair around my finger.

He paused for a minute rubbing his temple before taking a seat at the bar. "Are you all right?" I asked.

"Yea, I'm fine, just feeling a tad bit dizzy." He lifted his glass in the air as if he were examining it. "The bartender must have made this drink stronger than the others." He stated firmly as I heard the drunkenness in his voice. "How about I take you up on your offer and we can get out of her now? Whose place are we headed to, mine or yours?"

"I think we should go to yo' place, only 'cause my nosey sister is in town and she's staying with me."

"Sounds good to me," he stated with a devilish smile upon his face. He just didn't know that he was in for a rude awakening.

I excused myself from him, by telling him, I had to go to the ladies room to powder my nose. Upon my return, he grabbed me by my waist and we walked out the door and headed to his crib.

Walking into his house, it looked like I just stepped in one of the cribs from MTV. Lucky was living large. I've never been in a house like his before. Comparing my house to his is like comparing a Honda Civic to a Mercedes Benz. There was definitely no comparison when it came to the two. He walked me up a long flight of stairs leading to the master bedroom. We sat on his bed talking and getting to know each other. He seemed like he was a cool cat. I found out through our conversation that he was a married man, but he and his wife are in the process of a messy divorce. He also has twelve kids by 10 different women, two of them by his soon to be ex-wife, and he's the oldest of his mother seven children. Talking to him, I found myself getting attracted to him, but I had to keep in mind that this was a job and I couldn't be attached to the target. "Money over Niggas" is the slogan that popped in my head.

I started thinking about how easy it is to seduce a man so I was really considering being a part of the team on a permanent basis. All you need is a cute face and a phat ass. My thoughts were interrupted when I felt Lucky's hand rubbing my thigh. His manly touch felt so good to me causing my body to quiver. His touched seemed so innocent. I closed my eyes and enjoyed the moment because I haven't been touched by a man in days. It was something about Lucky that caused him to have my undivided attention.

"I have a li'l surprise for you," I told him, as I

licked his earlobe in between words.

"Surprise for me?"

"Yea, do you not like surprises?"

"I love surprises, but why would you want to surprise me with anything, we just met?"

"Only because I can tell you are a hardworking man and you deserve the best." I said stroking his ego. "You are a man who appreciates good quality when it comes to women and I just want to show you a good time. Who knows what the future may hold for us and I just want to leave you with a good first impression of me." I could tell he was shocked by my responses and I had him eating out of the palm of my hands.

"Damn," was all I heard him say.

I needed to loosen up. "Do you have anything to drink?" I asked while standing up and unzipping the side of my jumpsuit.

He stated, "Yes," without any hesitation. "Is Grey Goose okay?"

"Yes, sweetie, Grey Goose would do just fine. There's nothing better than some Grey Goose to get me loose."

Earlier at the club, I spiked his drink when he had his eyes glued to Buttah's ass. I guess I didn't put enough in his drink because his ass is still conscience. I thought he would have been out for the count after telling me he was feeling dizzy.

Lucky proceeded downstairs to get us something to drink. When he returned, he had a chilled bottle of Grey Goose and two glasses in his hands. Instantly, his eyes widened. He almost dropped the two glasses and the bottle of Goose when he saw me on his oversized, custom, plush bed, asshole naked and Buttah standing in the bathroom doorway, asshole naked.

"Surprise," I yelled. He was speechless. He wasn't expecting this at all. Instantly, he sat the glasses and liquor on a table next to the bed and started taking off his clothes. Looking at him, you would have thought he was in some type of contest that required him to remove his clothes. He removed his clothes so damn fast. He didn't even inquire how she got in or how I knew her. All he saw was two Brazilian waxed pussies and he wanted in.

"This is my type of party," he shouted.

"Hi, daddy," Buttah politely spoke while gliding her finger in and out of her mouth then rubbing her hand across he hard nipples. "We are going to have a good time, but first, can you get me a glass so we can toast to us?"

Buttah walked over to where he was, with her four-inch hot pink pumps on and stopped dead in front of him. She purposely bent over, revealing nothing but ass, picking his clothes up off the floor. His dick had to grow about 10 inches in a matter of seconds. He was instantly turned on and so was I. His dick was hard as a rock and stood straight up with a curve at the tip. He eagerly ran back downstairs to get another glass. I couldn't wait until he got back so I could feel him inside of me. Why let a big dick like that go to waste?

Buttah walked over to me, spread my legs apart, and let her tongue massage my clit. That girl really knows how to please me. Licking on me made me forget about all the stuff she had ever done to hurt me. I can't believe that I am addicted to her tongue. I will have her licking the pussy over any man any day. She wrote the alphabets on my pussy with her tongue, which normally causes me to cum at the letter S. She never got a chance to get to that letter because at L we heard a loud thumping sound coming from down stairs like someone had just hit the floor. I pushed Buttah's head from between my legs. I quickly started gathering my things because I didn't know what was taking place down stairs. I wasn't sure if he had finally passed out from me spiking his drink or if someone had knocked him out. I looked over at Buttah and she was cracking up laughing.

"Bitch, what's funny?" I said angrily, now standing face to face with her.

"If you could have seen the scared look on your face, you would be cracking up laughing also. This is all a part of the game. One of my brother's workers just knocked Lucky ass out. What you heard was him hitting the floor. They came in the house after I came in. Just like you left the door open for me, I left the door open for them. I guess when he went back downstairs they saw that as the perfect opportunity to make their move."

"So what's next?"

"Just follow my lead."

When Lucky regained conscience, we all were tied up to a chair, still naked, staring at men with Tony Montana masks covering their faces.

"You know what we are here for so just give it up."

"I don't know what you're talking about."

One of the dudes pointed the gun at Lucky's dick and said, "If you wanna be able to continue to fuck these two pretty, young thangs you have here or any other bitch, you better stop playing with us and give us the money."

Right away, I started crying. It wasn't an act. I was scared shitless. Buttah didn't tell me guns were going to be involved. I thought we were just going to spike his drink and when he woke up everything he owned would be gone. One can only assume, but seeing is believing.

"Bitch, shut up with all that crying," one of the guys shouted. I couldn't believe what was going on. Are these guys with us or against us? Why are they yelling at me? I couldn't control my tears so one of the fake Tony Montana's came and smacked the shit out of me. More tears began to flow down my face, but this time I kept the noise down. I was crying a river. While sniffling and trying to calm down, I looked at Buttah to see if she showed any signs of sympathy for me and I didn't see any. From the look on her face, it seemed like she enjoyed watching me be slapped. I think I even noticed a slight smirk on her face. Then, out of nowhere, dude punched Lucky in his facing demanding the money again.

"Okay, okay. The money is in the basement." I guess he couldn't take the abuse any longer so he gave in.

Lucky and the two guys walked out the room and down the flight of stairs leaving me and Buttah tied to our chairs. Before leaving out the room, Lucky looked at us with pure evil in his eyes as if to say, "I know you bitches set me up." I didn't say a word, I just stared back at him trying to plead to him with my eyes that I didn't have anything to do with this, but it seems as if he knew my eyes were lying.

"It's almost over." Buttah said eagerly as soon as the others left the room and was out of listening range, while squirming her way out of the rope. I couldn't believe this shit went down like it did. I was expecting something totally different. I guess there is never any plan; you just go with the flow. I was happy that it was almost over. I just wanted to go back to the hotel, have a drink, and forget this day ever happened. As Buttah was untying me, we heard gunshots.

Chapter Twenty-Two
HONEYBUN

*L*istening to my iPod and packing my clothes was a breath of fresh air for me. I really needed to get away from Chicago to clear my mind of Nino. I know eventually Nino was going to come looking for me, but in the meantime, I was going to enjoy my trip.

I haven't been out of town in a while and I was excited to get back in the business. I also loved the thrill that comes alone with setting these good-for-nothing ass niggas up. Believe me, if any nigga had the chance to get money the way we do, they wouldn't have any problems with setting our asses up. They wouldn't even second guess setting a female up who was checking major bread in the streets. Niggas set each other up all the time, but we just doing it a smarter way with pussy as bait.

Packing my bags seemed like it was taking for-

ever. I was only going be gone to the Big Apple for the
weekend, but a girl could never over pack. I wished that
both jobs were in the same state because I know I'm
going to be bored until I get the phone call to go and
attack my prey. I'm quite sure Buttah and Sparkle are
having fun in ATL. Hopefully, next time, we can all
travel together.

My flight was scheduled to leave the next
morning at 8:30 a.m. That gives me just enough time to
spend with Kane before I leave. I miss him dearly. I haven't seen him in three days because he had to drive to
High Point, North Carolina to see his daughter graduate
from college. Sometimes I hate he's that old because I
feel that our age difference will definitely cause some
type of conflict with me and his children. When he told
me that two of his daughters and I are the same age, all
I could muster up to say was, "Wow."

I spoke with Kane briefly over the phone and
told him that I needed to see him. We agreed to meet at
the lake-front within the hour. When I arrived, he was
already there. I spotted him as soon as I pulled in the
parking lot. He was the only black stallion in sight. I got
out the car and damn near ran to where he was because I missed him just that much. I walked up slowly
behind him and wrapped my arms around his body.

"Hey beautiful," he stated.

"Hey baby I replied," kissing him on the back of
his neck. It was something about this man that had me
open. I know I just got out of a fucked up relationship

and shouldn't be trying to start another one, but he seemed so genuine, different, and right. When I'm around him, he brightens up my day and helps me forget all the pain that I've endured with Nino.

Kane finally turned around and greeted me with a peck on my lips. He grabbed my hand and we walked up and down the beach for what seemed like hours intrigued in each other's conversations. Being in his presence made me want to change my mind about going out of town, but I couldn't let him sidetrack me. There was money to be made and I couldn't see myself in the same situation I just got out of which was depending on a man.

"Kane, I know you just got back in town and you were expecting to spend some quality time with me, but I received a devastating phone call earlier today from my cousin. She told me that my mom's only sister died of breast cancer and they need me to fly out first thing tomorrow morning because the funeral is Saturday." My head was held down the whole time I was telling him the lie. I couldn't dare stare him in his eyes and lie to him. He put his hand on my chin to lift my head up. Once my eyes met his eyes, a single tear fell down my face. I didn't know why I was crying because my mom didn't even have a sister. Kane stepped in closer to me and licked my tears away as they fell one by one down my face.

"I'm sorry to hear that baby. If you want, I will fly out with you." Damn, he got me with that one; I wasn't expecting his ass to want to tag along.

"No, baby, I'll be fine. I'm only going to be gone for a couple of days."

Kane hugged me tightly as if this was going to be his last time ever laying his eyes on me. We walked down the lake front for about five more minutes until we came across a stoop. We sat down for what seemed like hours, without saying a word, staring into space. He grabbed my hand and held it tightly as we admired the night sky while the cool breeze from the night water hit our bodies. The moment we were sharing together was amazing. He leaned in to get closer to me. He wrapped his hands around my small waist, forcing our bodies together. Seconds later, his soft, firm lips were touching mine and he kissed me passionately as our tongues met each other's like magnets. His hands explored every inch of my body until he reached my love spot and a slight moan escaped my mouth, causing me to blush. Kane's hands continued to explore my love spot, causing my moans to become more intense as he rubbed my clitoris. *I've been craving this moment from the first time we met.* He looked deeply into my eyes and asked if I wanted him to stop. I shook my head no. Kane continued rubbing my clit as I slid out of my pants. As my naked ass hit the cold stoop, reality hit me. I was outside about to get my back blown out. I wasn't comfortable with having sex outside, but the setting was perfect, with the moon and stars above. He told me to lie on my back and I did as I was told. I stared into the night sky and I knew he was about to take me to ecstasy. Upon lowering himself one stoop below me, he spread my legs as far as they would go. His face was drawn to my love spot and his tongue met my clitoris. Between each lick and each peck he asked me was I all his. How could I say no? Hell yea I was his.

With every lick to my pussy, my body shook from the pleasure. The tingling sensation had my body in overdrive. I knew I was about to cum so I started screaming stop in between moans. My body was ready to explode, but my mind was telling me something else. He obeyed me and made his way up to the upper part of my body. He pulled my shirt over my head and began to suck on my nipples one by one, then both at a time. Again Kane whispered in my ear and asked me "Honey-bun, are you all mines," and I answered once again "yes" without any hesitation. He began to lick his way back down south while kissing every inch of my body, never missing a spot. He licked from my neck, to my stomach, to my thighs, and then back to my clitoris. Kane's old ass knew how to work his tongue no doubt about that and I was enjoying every moment of it. As he sucked on my pussy, he inserted two fingers inside of me then I exploded. The sensation I felt from that orgasm had a bitch out of breath and ready to collapse at any given moment. He took my shirt, wiped my juices away, and then gave me the shirt off his back.

"Let's go to my place." Kane said, penis now fully erect.

"Lead the way."

Kane jumped in his car and I jumped in mine, but instead of going to his place, he stopped at the first hotel he saw. On the way, I browsed through the radio stations until I found something relaxing to listen to. I listened attentively as Jennifer Holiday sang her heart out to some nigga telling him that he was going to love her. I giggled to myself because I was determined to have Kane love me. I reached between my legs and massaged my clit with one hand while the other hand continued to drive. All I wanted now was for this pussy to be wet and ready for him.

As soon as we made our way through the hotel room door, we both started undressing immediately. When his pants dropped to the floor, my eyes bucked because his dick was the size of the snake from the movie Anaconda. We walked through the hotel suite kissing and rubbing all over each other until we reached the small kitchenette. I must admit he had the biggest dick I ever seen. His strong arms lifted my body and placed me on the kitchen counter. Placing one hand behind my neck and forcing my neck to lean to one side, he began to kiss me aggressively. He worked his way from my neck down to my love spot, making sure I was extremely wet. Upon completing his task, he inserted his manhood inside of me. I damn near jumped out my skin. I screeched out from the pain. With every stroke, the pain subsided and pleasure was soon to follow. He took his time with me and made sure I felt comfortable. I didn't want the night to end, but I knew I had an early flight the next morning. After sex, we headed to the bed and laid in it for a while then we took a shower together to freshen up. I put his shirt back on and my pants, but left the underwear to give him something to think about while I was gone. He walked me to the door and we said our goodbyes.

$$$$$$$$$

When I woke up the clock read 6:00a.m. I could have shitted bricks. I couldn't believe I was running late. I'm supposed to arrive at the airport two hours before my flight leaves, but it doesn't look like that's going to happen. I quickly washed my face, brushed my teeth, and threw on a pair of shorts and a t-shirt, then headed out the door. I'm praying the airport isn't crowed so I won't miss my flight. I'm glad I've already packed and took a shower. When I walked out the door to head to my car, Kane was outside waiting.

"What are you doing here?" I asked, smiling continuously.

"I came to take my baby to the airport. I know you had a long night, and I thought you probably weren't in the mood to drive, so therefore I came to be your personal driver."

"How sweet," I blurted out. He grabbed my luggage and we headed to the airport.

$$$$$$$$$

Arriving in New York brought a smile to my

face because I knew there was money to be made and
money to be spent. I checked into The Chatwal Hotel
right off 44th street. Upon walking into the room, I was
blown away. J-Boogie had me set up in a nice ass suite.
The floors were marble, just the way I liked it. I hated
going to hotels with carpet on the floor. All types of
bacteria could be caught in it. There were flat screen
TV's in every room including the bathroom. Actually,
the bathroom was the sexiest part of the suite. It had
his-and-her sinks with granite counter top and his-
and-her toilets. *Damn, I wish Kane was here.* It had a
separate shower from the bath and the cutest decora-
tions hung on the wall. Walking out the bathroom into
the bedroom had me fantasizing about the type of damage Kane could have done to my love spot if he was
here with me. The bed was an oversized heart-shaped
bed with a canopy above it. To the left of the bed was a
perfect size Jacuzzi that seats two.

After unpacking my clothes, I heard a knock on
my door and it startled me. I didn't know anyone in
New York so my mind was puzzled. *Who could this be?*
I tiptoed toward the door and peaked through the peep
hole only to come to realization that it had to be room
service. After opening the door, I was even more
shocked by the person in front of me.

"What's up, shawty?" J-boogie said, as he
marched his way through the door.

"I wasn't expecting to see you here. I thought I
was only going to communicate with you over the

phone."

"You know I couldn't let my favorite girl roam the dangerous streets of New York City by herself. I know this is your first day back on the job and I wanted you to feel as comfortable as possible since Buttah's not here with you. I know you don't need me to hold your hand, but I just need to be the one to come to your rescue if anything goes wrong."

"What could possibly go wrong?" I asked with a crazy look on my face.

"Honeybun, you can never be too careful with these New Yorkers, especially this nigga Money. He's one of the slickest niggas out here, and he's on point at least ninety percent of the time."

"If Money is such a threat and on point at all times, why are we even on this job?"

"Like I said, he's on point ninety percent of the time not a hundred percent. I've been watching him, learning his strengths and weaknesses for months, and I know with you on my team we can definitely take him down."

"Just make sure you are close by incase anything does goes wrong. 'Cause just like you said, these New Yorkers are slick as hell."

"Baby girl, you know I will never let anything happen to you in this city. I gotcha back. Just keep in mind there's a lot of money to be made and he's one of the riches niggas on the east coast. One more thing, your stay here might be longer than the weekend because we have to make our moves wisely."

"Damn," I said aloud, not really wanting it to escape my mouth.

"What's wrong, love?"

"Nothing at all," I stared at him with a crazy look on my face.

"Believe me it will be worth your while," he said while rubbing his hand alongside my arm.

His touch felt so good, it actually brought back old memories. I missed him so much. On the other hand, was I just going through a phase that all women go through when getting out of a relationship, which is fuck anything they see as if it was going to get their ex mad. Even though we dated years ago and he did me wrong, I was still attracted to him. Any woman that was into men would be attracted to his thuggish sexy ass. He was the perfect height, had small, yet full lips, with skin as smooth as a baby's ass. I know he did me wrong back in the day, but I'm a semi-single woman out of town with a single man in a bomb ass hotel suite, something was liable to go down between us.

"How do you like the room?"

"I love the room." I said as I stared into his eyes and leaned in for a kiss. He didn't stop me. He kissed me back. I think he had this all planned out. That's why I have this extravagant room. One thing led to another and next thing I know, I was on the heart shaped bed taking his dick from the back. My pussy was still throbbing from the previous night I had with Kane, but I had to have him. With Kane it was love making. With J-Boogie, it was a fuck. He gave it to me rough and hard.

After we were finished sweating and catching our breath, we lay in bed and talked about Money. He told me that he wanted me to have a "coincidental" run in with him that afternoon. He showed me pictures of him so I could know what to expect. Money was this plus size dude. He looked like he weighed anywhere between 350lbs and 400lbs. He was all fat and no muscle. His belly hung over his pants. I could only imagine what he's working with between his fat ass thighs. I'm praying I don't have to sleep with him just to get what we need. He looks so damn disgusting.

"Money eats at this restaurant called Destiny's every day at 3:00p.m. The only thing you have to do is put your charm on him. Swing your ass in his face a couple of times and you will have him in the palm of your hands. I told Buttah to give you this particular job because you are more his type."

"Type, are you kidding me? His fat ass has a type. Who would have imagined.

The next day I got right down to business. I knew for a fact that the niggas from New York like sexy, yet ghetto chicks, therefore I had to dress in the best ghetto threads my money could buy, Kimora Lee Simmon's (Baby Phat). Arriving at the restaurant, I strutted my phat ass into the restaurant and scanned the area until I found my prey. I had my hair pulled in a pony-tail with a Chinese bang like Keisha wore from the movie Belly. I was also rocking a pair of bamboo earrings with my name in it and chewing on bubble gum. My feet were complimented by a fresh pair of Air Force Ones.

Scanning the room, I noticed an empty table directly across from his. I made my way to the table and dropped my purse purposely before sitting down. "Shit," I cursed out loud, bending over giving him nothing, but a view of my perfect round ass while giggling to myself. When I sat down, I noticed him smiling at me, seeing nothing but all thirty-two of his dingy white teeth.

"Heeeeey, sexy," he shouted from his table.

"Hey sexy," I spoke back not meaning a word I was saying.

"You not from around here are you?" he asked.

"To answer your question no, is it that obvious? How could you tell?" I said while walking to his table.

"It's yo' booty; I mean, your beauty that stands out. I know with a face like yours you couldn't be from 'round this way."

"Can I take a seat?" I asked not waiting for an answer, but sitting down anyway. "I'm actually from Indiana. I'm here for my aunt's funeral." I used the lie I told Kane.

"Sorry to hear that sexy. So, how long you gonna be in town?"

I wanted to say, "As long as it takes to set your fat stupid ass up," but I decided against that. "I'm only gonna be here for the weekend."

"Well that doesn't give me that much time to spend with you now does it?"

"I guess it doesn't," I stated. "By the way what's your name? I'm Trice." I said while reaching my hand out to shake his. I never give a nigga my government name or my real nick name when I'm out of town doing a job. Even though my earrings said my government name, he was too busy watching my ass to notice what the earrings said.

"Mine's is Money. I'm only assuming that you're having lunch with me since you are already sitting down."

"Yea you assumed right, and me being the type of woman I am, lunch is on me," I stated as I twirled my finger around a piece of my phony pony."

"I like yo' style, ma, but I would be less of a man if I let you pay for our meal."

"No I insist."

"Okay, well, since you insist, I guess dinner is on me."

"Fine, sounds like a plan."

Money and I sat and had lunch together. His fat ass knows he can throw back some plates. He wasn't trying to hold anything back. Immediately after eating, he asked me if I had anything to wear to the funeral and I told him no. I had plans to go shopping after lunch. He told me that he would love to escort me to the mall because he wanted to get to know me a little better before I went back home. Mission one accomplished!

Chapter Twenty-Three
Bone

*S*itting in my spacious living room and staring at the ceiling, I was contemplating on what my next move was going to be. I can't let either one of those conniving bitches get away with playing with a nigga's heart. After seeing the DVD my brother had, the only thing I had on my mind when it came to Sparkle was revenge. She definitely has to pay for sleeping with Marcus. She betrayed me fully and the only thing that I had on my mind when it came to Buttah was trying to get her back in my life.

After doing a little more thinking and asking my brother some questions. I found out that Buttah and I wasn't sleeping around with each other when the tape was made so she gets a pass on this one. If I play my cards right, I can have them both and come out on top. I can blackmail Buttah into sleeping with me by telling her that I will tell Sparkle about us and getting Sparkle in my life for revenge wouldn't be a hard task to accomplish because she still wants me.

I sat in the dark a little while longer, in deep thought, smoking a blunt and drinking a glass of Ciroc, thinking about the two women. One whom I was trying to destroy and the other I wanted in my life. I reached in my Diesel jeans for my phone and called Sparkle to try to persuade her back into my life. I dialed her seven digital, blocking my number, only because I knew she was upset about seeing me and her girl together.

"Talk."

"Hey, my perfect little angel," I tried to sound as sincere as possible as soon as she picked up the phone.

"Who this?" I heard her speak as she chewed on something in between each word. By the tone of her voice, I could tell she had one hand on her hip with her lips poked out being the ghetto-chick that she is.

"Stop acting like you don't know who this is."

"How you figure this an act nigga? First, you call my phone blocked and now you expecting me to know who the hell you are off GP. If you don't tell me who the hell I'm speaking with, I'm gonna hang up the phone," she stated, with an automatic attitude.

"Stop playing with me. You know this Bone."

"Bone, umm...umm...Bone who?" I noticed the bitch trying to be sarcastic. Now since she wants to act like she doesn't know who the fuck I am, the more she plays with me, the worse off she's making her situation.

I cut to the chase. "If you want to hear an apology, I apologize. That was the sole purpose of this call."

"So are you admitting to sleeping with Buttah?"

"No, I'm not admitting to anything because that never happened. I wouldn't do you like that. You're my girl and she's your girl. I know what she done to you in the past. All you saw me doing was lending a helping hand. She was stranded and I was happy to help one of your friends. All I'm apologizing for is cutting you out my life the way I did. I was going through something at the time. My situation then would not have allowed me to love you the way you deserved to be loved. I felt it wouldn't be fair to you if I continued seeing you knowing that I wasn't able to give you 100% percent of me. You're a good woman Sparkle and I need you in my life." She was soaking up every word that I shot at her like a sponge. I heard her sniffle in between each word that I spoke as they rolled off my tongue. Right then and there, I knew I had her.

"Bone, you should have told me. I would have understood. I wouldn't have cared if you couldn't give me a 100% of you. I was willing to accept 40% or 50% as long as I had you in my life."

"Baby you deserve the best and I wanted you to have all of me, not some to me. I hope that you can accept my apology. I love you Sparkle and I don't think I will ever stop loving you. Do you think we can go out to dinner later on tonight? There is a lot we need to talk about."

"I would love to have dinner with you, but tonight is not a good night. I'm out of town visiting my family, but as soon as I get back in town I'll call you."

"Sounds like a plan to me, and remember Sparkle I love you."

I knew getting Sparkle back under my wings was going to be a piece of cake. She's so naïve. What I have in store for her she would never see coming. She is going to regret ever sleeping with my brother or any other man behind my back. Now it's time to call Buttah.

Ring... Ring... Ring...

There was no answer. I cursed myself repeatedly for falling in love with her. I called her phone several more time, and I still didn't get an answer. I wonder what the hell she could be doing that she can't pick up the phone and plus I haven't seen her leave her crib in a couple of days. Yes, I've been stalking her crib. I need Buttah in my life. I'm not understanding why I can't shake these feelings I have for her. I was very persistent with calling her. I wasn't going to stop until she picked up the phone. After several more attempts, she finally picked up.

"What the hell do you want?" She whispered in the phone.

"I miss you. I need to see you. Why haven't you been picking up your phone? Where are you?"

"Bone, I don't have to answer your questions. We are not a couple, so can you please stop calling my phone."

"No Buttah, listen to me and listen attentively. I'm not gonna stop calling 'cause you belong to me and every time I call, you better pick up. I don't have time to be playing any games with you 'cause tricks are for kids. If you don't start spending time with me, Sparkle is gonna find out about our sexcapade and I know for a fact that you don't want that to happen; now do you?"

"I can't believe you Bone. Why are you doing this? I don't wanna continue to hurt Sparkle."

"You should've thought about that before you started flirting with me. It's not over 'til I say it's over so tonight I need to see you at my place with nothing on, but pumps and a trench coat. No panties or bra, just pure skin."

"Please Bone, can you just walk away. Let's not hurt Sparkle more than what we have already done."

"There's no walking away and if you don't wanna see her hurt, I'll see you tonight. Our secret is our little secret 'til you cross me."

I hung up the phone feeling like I accomplished the second part of my goal, but immediately after I hung up the phone it rang. Buttah number flashed across my blackberry screen. I didn't pick up because I didn't want to hear any excuses. I hit the end button and sent her straight to voicemail.

Chapter Twenty-Four
BUTTAH

*W*ho in the hell does Bone think he is giving me a damn ultimatum? There's no way I'll be able to make it to his house tonight. I paced the hotel hallway floor back and forth thinking about my current situation and how I really fucked up this time by getting pregnant.

I picked the phone up to call Bone, but he didn't answer. Calling him back to back had me really agitated, but I wouldn't and couldn't let up. I guess he figured it was his way or no way. I continued calling his phone because I had to let him know that I was out of town and that I wouldn't be able to make it to his house tonight.

Ring...Ring... Ring....

I called his phone one last time, and again it

went to voicemail. This time I decide to leave him a message. "Bone, this...you know who the fuck this is. I'm calling yo' stupid ass back to let you know I won't be able to make it tonight 'cause I'm out of town, so don't wait up; holla."

Letting Bone have the best of me was not an option at this point. I needed to come up with a plan. I can't let no man control my life especially him. He can't make me be with him if I don't want to. I hate him, I hate him, I hate him, but for now, I guess I got to do what he says until I'm able to figure out how to get rid of him.

After leaving the voicemail on Bone's phone, I headed back to the hotel room. Sparkle and I discussed the incident that took place at Lucky's house. All I'm going to say is that his parents definitely have one less son to worry about. One of my brother's workers told me that in the process of Lucky opening the safe to retrieve the money, he came out with a gun shooting and one of them got shot in the arm. The other worker shot back without any hesitation hitting him directly in the chest causing his spirit to be relieved from its temporarily home.

When I heard the gun shots come from the basement, my adrenaline started pumping. I guess that was the gangsta in me ready to come out. I have my share of war stories. Momma didn't raise a punk. There have been plenty of times I didn't want my brother involved in my bullshit so I handle the situations myself rather it was with a nigga or a bitch. It's something about a chromed out gun, the sound of gun shots, and the smell of gun powder that takes me to another level.

We didn't find any drugs in the house, but we managed to get away with two hundred thousand dollars. I wasn't expecting him to have that much money in his house but lucky for us. The nigga was loaded. The safe in the basement that was made into the floor only had ten thousand in it, but we knew there were more. Each bedroom in the house contained a safe. It took us a while to find each safe because the safes were mounted in different locations. Either it was mounted in the floor or in the wall behind a picture frame. We search the house for what seemed like hours until we were satisfied with the amount of money we obtained. Lucky was the type of nigga that didn't trust the banks or anyone else with his money so we knew it was more to the first safe.

"You all right?" I asked Sparkle, even though I knew that she wasn't.

"Do I look all right, Buttah? I had no idea someone was going to get killed in the process of all this."

"I didn't know either, but shit happens."

"Shit happens. Is that all you can say?"

"Hell yea that's all I can say 'cause shit does happens. Either you get with the program or are gone. There's a lot of money to be made in this line of work. If you don't want part of this get rich money scheme just let me know 'cause there are other bitches out here that are willing to take your place and if the next bitch don't want to be down then that leaves more money for me." The more I spoke, the more I could see the animosity being built up with Sparkle's toward me, but I didn't care because I was determined to get my point across. "I'm not gonna babysit your grown ass. One minute it seems like you down for the mighty dollar and the next minute you acting like you not. Make yo' mind up, girl."

"It's not about being down for the mighty dollar. A man's life has been taken on the account of us. Don't you have a conscience?"

"Nope, I don't have a conscience 'cause having a conscience will keep me broke for the rest of my life or get me killed. If you want to live like I'm living, you better get with the program or be gone like I said before."

I know what I said to her was harsh, but what we were doing has to be taking seriously because if we don't take it serious our life could be next. Maybe she isn't cut out for this line of work like I thought. Maybe all she is good for is spreading her legs for a couple of dollar. In a way, I felt somewhat bad that she had to go through this on her first job, but now she know sometimes she can expect the worst of the worst.

We talked about the situation some more in depth for what seemed like hours, but after a while, she began to see things from my point of view. I knew once she saw her pay for the day her mind would change 100%.

$$$$$$$$$

Once back in Chicago we went our separate ways. It felt so good to be home. She walked away with $30,000. Who makes that type of money putting in a couple days of work? I wonder what she's going to do with her pay. Frankly, I don't care what she does with her money because she is the least of my concern.

Back at my condo, I poured myself a glass of orange juice. I sat and thought for the first time about the child that was growing inside of me. Once again, the thought of me telling Bone entered my mind, but quickly vanished. There is no way I was going to tell him. I stared at myself in my living room mirror and noticed my face was getting fatter and rounder. So much has been going on with me that I kept forgetting to call the abortion clinic.

"Hi Sarah, my name is Butt..." I had to catch myself I was about to give her my street name instead of my government name. "My name is Savannah; I was calling because I want to terminate my pregnancy."

"How long are you into your pregnancy?"

Good question I thought to myself. "I'm about two month."

I said not sure of my answer.

I heard her flipping through what seems like an appointment book "My next available appointment date is next week on the 10th. I have a 9, 10, 12, and 3 o'clock available, which one is convenient for you.

"You can pencil me in for the 3 o'clock," I stated trying to sound professional.

"Okay. One more quick question for your, are you staying awake for the procedure or are you being put to sleep? Before you answer the question let me inform you there's a $100.00 difference in the price."

I was offended by that statement, but kept my composure because she didn't know me from a can of paint. I wanted to yell, "Bitch, $100.00 ain't shit to me. I go through money like babies go through clothes. I could buy yo' $5 ass if I wanted to," but I responded politely. "I think I'll be getting put to sleep."

"All right, then make sure you have someone pick you up because you won't be able to drive because of the medication. You will still feel a little drowsy when you wake up. Don't forget to bring your I.D and if you have insurance bring that card also.

Once off the phone with the abortion clinic, I began to feel a lot better. Even though this was my first pregnancy, I felt no connection with the fetus growing inside of me. It's a strong possibility that if I were pregnant by someone else I would feel some type of connection with my child. Getting rid of this baby should have been the first thing on my to-do-list.

Later on that day I headed over to Bone's house only because I didn't want any trouble out of him. When I walked in his apartment the first thing he asked, "Are you pregnant?" *What the fuck is the nigga a mind reader. How could he possibly know?*

"Hell motherfuckin' naw. I'm not pregnant. Why would you ask me a stupid ass question like that?"

"'Cause you glowing and your face is fuller and rounder than before. I received a call from my mom earlier today saying that she had a dream about fish and you know how that ol' sayin' goes." He stated with a fatherly smile upon his face.

"Fuck that ol' saying. Like I said ain't nobody pregnant. I just eat too much and the food has finally caught up with me."

"If you're not pregnant, then you want mind pissing on this stick then."

I can't believe this shit. What nigga you know have a pregnancy test lying around their house? Bone is really tripping. "Are you really expecting me to piss on that stick? If I'm telling yo' black ass I'm not pregnant; why won't you just believe me?"

"Buttah, I don't believe anything you say out yo' mouth, especially when it comes to something like this." He stated as he stared me straight into my eyes.

He handed me a glass of water and told me to drink up so I could get the urge to go to the bathroom. I didn't obey. I place the glass down on the kitchen counter. I shouldn't have done that because that pissed him off. He then lifted the glass of water back off the counter and threw it in my face.

"What the fuck..." I yelled while wiping my face with my shirt. He then walked over to the kitchen sink and filled the glass back up with water. The only thing I kept saying in my head was why did I come over here in the first place? Bone placed the glass back down in front of me, never taking his eyes off me. I will admit at that point I was scared out my damn mind. With Bone's obsession over me, anything was liable to take place. Never taking his eyes off me, I guess he was waiting for me to pick the glass back up, but I didn't budge. Still staring me down, he quickly grab me by my neck. With his free hand, he picked the glass up off the counter and forced the water down my throat. Bone filled the glass back up several more time until I told him I had to go to the bathroom.

Still scared out my mind, I didn't know what his reaction was going to be when the test came back positive. I went in the bathroom and tried closing the door, but he wasn't having that. He kicked the door back open as quickly as it closed. As he stood in the doorway watching me like a hawk, I ripped open the pregnancy box and sat it on the sink.

Pulling my pants down I sat on the cold toilet seat getting ready to take the pressure off my bladder. Moving in slow motion, I took the small cup from the box so I can urine in it. Nervous as one could be, I started shaking like a leaf on a breezy fall night. The only thing that kept playing in my head is how in the hell did I get myself in this fucked up situation? Placing the cup back on the sink, Bone quickly placed the stick into the cup with a huge smile upon his face. Once again my mind went to wondering and all I could think at that point was my life is over. One minute seem like one hour, two minutes seems like a week, and three minutes seem like months. When the three minutes was finally up, Bone smile quickly was replaced with a frown, and my frown was replaced with a smile. The test came back negative. How the hell did that happened. I don't know and didn't care. All I could say to him was, "I told yo' crazy ass I wasn't pregnant, now get the fuck out my face." Bone was so full of rage he didn't say a word he just turned and left out the bathroom.

Chapter Twenty-Five
NINO

"Boss man, there haven't been a soul going in or out the house in a couple of days. I don't know where this bitch at. Her car is here, but there are no signs of life inside that house. The damn lights haven't even come on."

"Aye, li'l homie, are you sure?"

"Hell yea, I'm sure boss man. I've been watching this bitch house like a watch dog.

"All right, Twon, you put in enough work. Call one of the other homies and tell him to post up. Eventually she'll pop back up, but under no circumstance is that house to go unwatched."

"One love, I'll hit you later boss.

"One."

Being highly disappointed that Honeybun was nowhere to be found only added fuel to the fire. Honestly, I never thought it would ever get to this point with her. Honeybun beat me with a bat, stabbed me, shot at me, stole my money, sold my car, and put my house up for sale. I'll be less of a man if there were no consequences that followed. What she has to know is every action causes a reaction. She knows what's best for her; that's why she hasn't been home. I hate I just didn't go in the house blasting her ass when I had the opportunity. Instead, I used the wrong head and now I'm left wondering where she could be. Sitting at the crib pondering on it wasn't going to get me nowhere so I decided to get in my car to make a couple of runs.

Driving through the busy pm traffic, different scenes played out in my head on how I was going to kill Honeybun. No matter which one I decided on, her death wasn't going to be an easy one. She talks about how much she misses her mother I'm going to do her a favor and send her exactly to where her mother is.

Pulling up to the storage garage where I kept my cars, I was approached by the female clerk with a smile on her face. Why was she smiling at me, I had the slightest idea because she always gives me a hard time when I'm here. She disliked me because I wouldn't give her the time of day. She would throw herself at me constantly when I came to check on my cars only to get the cold shoulder from me in return.

"Hey Mr. Nino, how are you on this beautiful day?"

"I'm doing okay and you?" I stated trying to be

cordial with her.

"Are you here to pick up your last car? I'm
gonna miss seeing your face around here."

"What you talking about my last car?" I know
I'm not a genius, but I do know simple math. I had five
fucking cars here; Honeybun sold one, which leaves me
with four cars to check on.

"Your wifey has been coming by with some
handsome man getting your cars out of storage. She
said that you all were about to move out of town and
that y'all were selling the cars. Since you are here today,
I figured that you were coming to pick up your last
car," she giggled as she let the words rotate off her
tongue.

"You got to be kidding me," I shouted in so
much rage and anger. Honeybun is really showing her
ass. With the new attitude, the clerk was giving me I
knew she knew exactly what Honeybun was up to. She
want me to probably feel the hurt that I blessed upon
her when I didn't give her the time of day, but that okay
fuck both of them bitches.

I called Twon and he met me at the storage garage to drive my car to another nearby storage. The car
that she left me had sentimental value to it. It was
passed down from my great grandfather. If she would
have sold this car, that would have equaled an automatic death sentence for her whole family.

Meanwhile, after leaving the storage garage, I
picked my money up off the block. I'm glad my workers

have been on top of their business because I didn't want to hurt them boys. They actually were good people, but just get side track by the ladies from time to time. Shortly after, I arrived at the mall to pick up a gift for Boo. Boo is the only person that understands me, this is why I love her so much. As I walked through the mall, I checked my phone every five minutes to make sure I didn't have any missed calls from the little homie that was scoping out Honeybun's house for me. She really has me on edge. Stopping at Jared's I purchased a nice engagement ring for Boo. I was ready to spend the rest of my life with her.

Chapter Twenty-Six
HONEYBUN

*E*ven though Money fat ass was on my side, I had a big ass smile across my face. The nigga dropped at least five g's on me when we went shopping. Not only did he buy me an outfit for the funeral, he bought me a seven day wardrobe made from the finest threads money could buy, with matching purses and shoes. He didn't take me shopping at the mall. He took me to the finest boutiques that New York has to offer.

After the make-believe funeral, I got up with Money. For the first couple of hours we were together, we rode around making several stops at different restaurants. Each restaurant he went into, he came out with a brown paper bag full of money. As I sat in the car and observed his actions, I texted J-Boogie to let him know what was going on. J-Boogie told me that he knew he had some type of illegal dealings going on inside those restaurants. I wasn't sure how much money was in each bag; what I did know was that we stopped at 10 restaurants before we made it to the hotel.

Gathering his bags and putting them into one black plastic bag, we headed into the hotel, walked right past the front desk and got on the elevator. When we arrived to the room, we chatted for a brief moment before Money excused himself out of the room along with the black plastic bag. I texted J the room number and the hotel address to where we were staying. When fat ass returned, he didn't have the bag in his hand anymore. This is where the shit gets tricky. Now I see this is what J was talking about. He told me that every time he followed Money, he always checked into a hotel with the moneybag, but always left the hotel with nothing in his hand. There was no way of him knowing who he dropped the money off to. He said each time he followed him, it would be a different hotel, but it was always the same routine as far as him picking up the money from the restaurants. We could have easily robbed him in traffic, but didn't want to cause a scene. This is why he needed me to get close to him to see what went on once he went inside the hotel, but from the looks of it, this going to be hard for me to find out.

As Money's eyes tried to undressed me, he shouted, "Li'l mama, you rocking that outfit that I bought you. How about we run to Victoria's Secret to get you some lingerie to model in for me?"

Taking off my clothes, one piece at a time, I revealed a black and red panty and bra set from Victoria's Secret, saying, "There's no need to go there 'cause I'm sure what I have on right now is just as sexy as what you are trying to buy me." I rubbed my hands along the curves of my body.

"Damn, baby, you look good as fuck. Where did you get all that ass from? Did you buy it?" He stated, while smacking my ass.

"Boy, you so silly," I said, giggling. "This ass here comes from greens and cornbread."

Feeling my bladder becoming full, I told Money to hold his thoughts until I came back from tinkling. With a smile on my face, I switched my phat ass in the bathroom, used it quickly, washed my hands, and came back out. When I crossed the threshold from the bathroom to the bed area, I felt a cold piece of steel against my head. Heart now beating rapidly, I knew things were not going as planned.

"Bitch, who the fuck are you?" He yelled, not caring who heard him.

"Calm down, Money, I'm Trice. I told you who I am. Why you tripping? And get that damn gun out my face," I stated calmly, smiling through the fear and knowing damn well I was about to shit on myself.

"You think this is a fucking joke, I see. This here ain't no joke. All I have to do is pull the trigger on this big motherfucker and you're dead," he stated, while snapping his fingers with his other hand for emphasis. I could be dead in a split second. "According to your ID, it says your name is Heidi and you live in Chicago, so stop with the lies, Trice, Heidi, whatever the fuck your name is."

I can't believe this fat motherfucker went through my purse.

"I'm gonna ask your pretty ass this question one more time and if you don't start talking soon, I'm gonna make sure you leave here in a body bag." My body temperature began to rise because I was nervous as hell. My left leg began to shake like I had to pee.

"Okay…okay…my name is Heidi, but everyone calls me Trice. That's my middle name. Why are you tripping over my name? It's just a name."

After I said my last sentence, he punched me in my face as if I was a nigga. I instantly balled up in the fetal position because I didn't want him to hit me again, but that didn't work. He grabbed me out the corner and began to beat my ass like Money Mayweather does his opponents. He beat my body so badly that I felt numb. I'm glad I already text J so I knew he would be there soon to save me from the 4X T-shirt wearing bastard. At that moment, it hit me, my phone was in my purse as well.

"So, you trying to set me up? Huh, bitch, who the fuck is J?" He stated, after his balled up fist repeatedly pecked my body.

"I don't know what you're talking about." I

knew I was caught, so no matter what I said at this point, I couldn't be saved. I was busted.

"You lying, conniving, dirty hoe," was all I heard before I blacked out.

$$$$$$$$$

Waking up three days later, I was happy to be alive. I woke up to my friends surrounding me with love. Buttah, Sparkle, and J-Boogie were there at my bedside. Buttah was the first person to speak to me. She hugged me with tears rolling down her cheeks. I had never seen Buttah so emotional before. I simply wiped her tears away and told her, "I'm alive, so don't cry." She has always walked around with an 'I don't give a fuck attitude,' but today, I saw another side of her that I thought didn't exist. Even though Sparkle and I didn't get along often, her presence made me realize she does have a heart after all. When she gave me a hug and a kiss, I knew this was a new beginning to a great friendship. I waited patiently for the last person in the room to give me a hug, but J-Boogie never moved or even acknowledged me and I knew why. He was hurt and distraught because he wasn't able to protect me.

I later found out that Money had shot me in my chest. According to Buttah, the doctor said he only missed my heart by a couple of inches. As badly as I wanted to seek revenge on Money, I didn't have it in me. At this point, I was just thankful to be alive and all I wanted to do was get out of New York and leave this behind me. I had a lot of unfinished business in the Chi that I needed to attend to.

There was a light knock on my room door as the door became ajar. "Can you all excuse us? I need to speak with Mrs. Heidi for a minute," the fine African American doctor said, as he walked into my room.

As they all left the room, they said they loved me and they were going to stop at the cafeteria to get something to eat and would be back soon.

"Hey, Dr. Greene," I spoke, hesitating a little before reading his name off his name tag. "What is it that you want to talk about?"

Pulling up a chair, the doctor flipped through some charts he had on his clipboard and said, "Heidi, you lost a lot of blood when you were shot. We had to test your blood to see what blood type you were in order to give you a blood transfusion."

"So, I had to get a blood transfusion?" I interrupted.

"Yes, Heidi. I'm not sure how long you were laid out in that hotel room before you were brought to the hospital, but from that chest shot alone you were really fighting for your life."

"But, I'm all good, right, doc," I stated, with concern in my voice.

"Not quite, this is why I need to talk to you." He stated in almost a whisper, "In the process of getting blood work from you," the doctor paused for a minute then continued, "there is no easy way to tell you this, but, Heidi, you are HIV positive."

"HIV, what you mean I have HIV? How could this be? I'm too pretty to have that ugly disease." My heart was so heavy that it felt like a ton of bricks was sitting on it. "What am I going to do, doc? Please tell me. Please tell me that y'all found a cure for this disease."

"I know this is a lot to take in, but just because you have HIV doesn't mean a death sentence. Many people have lived a normal live for many years with this disease. If you take care of yourself by taking the medicine properly, you can live a long time. I'm going to set you up with a clinic that I'm affiliated with back in your home town and I'm sure they will take care of you and educate you on what you're up against."

As the doctor continued to talk, my mind drifted to another place. All I kept saying was, "Why me?" The first person that came to mind was Nino's trifling ass. I know he was the one that gave this shit to me and now he must die.

$$\$\$\$\$\$\$\$\$\$$

"There's no place like home," I shouted, as I walked into my domain, which was once a happy home. A week has passed since the doctor came in my room and delivered the bad news. I wanted so badly to tell my friends what I was going through, but I was too ashamed and didn't want them to look at me differently. The fear that crossed my mind if J found out was nerve-wrecking. Even though J and I used protection, just the thought of him sleeping with me while I have this disease will make him go crazy.

Right when I thought my life was on the right track, this bomb is dropped on me. I can't continue to have a relationship with Kane. I can't look in his eyes and go on with him like I'm not dying and he may be, possibly, as well. Even though I had sex with Kane that one time, it was unprotected sex, so it's very possible that he contracted the disease as well.

As I did some cleaning around the house, I peeked out my window several times and noticed a car in front. I wondered who that could be. I never saw that car around here before. I grabbed my binoculars out of my closet to see who the guy was in front of my house. He didn't look familiar at all. I know he's been out there a long time because he had a whole pack of cigarette butts lying on the side of his car on the curb.

Panicking, I start dialing J-Boogie's number so he could come over because I thought Money had sent someone to finish the job of killing me. It dawned on me that my address on my ID was my old address when I used to live in the city, so I hung up the phone. Just to be on the safe side, I decided to get my gun and put it in my waistline as I continued to clean the house and think about how I was going to kill Nino.

Chapter Twenty-Seven
J-BOOGIE

I was full of rage as I punched a hole into the hotel wall when I kicked in the door and saw Honeybun laid out on the floor, shot. I called 911 quickly. I tried talking to her, but she wouldn't respond. I thought she was dead until I felt her pulse. Her pulse was beating faintly. I called 911 again and told them they better hurry the fuck up.

Once the ambulance arrived to get Honeybun, I was escorted to headquarters to be questioned. Sitting in the interrogation room, I felt like I was on an episode of Criminal Minds. They questioned me repeatedly with the same foolish questions, but changed the question around to make it seem like it was a different one. I knew who shot her, but I wasn't telling them shit. The police weren't going to have the opportunity of solving this case and sending it to court. In this case, I was the court of law and I sentence Money to death. He was going to die by my hands and nobody else's. Once the police realized they weren't going to get any answers out of me, they let me go.

Shortly after, I called Gunz and told him I needed him to fly to New York ASAP. At this point, I could care less about the money; I was out for blood. I was going to do to him what he tried to do to Honeybun.

I immediately filled Gunz in once I picked him up from the airport. Knowing he had a slight crush on Honeybun, I knew he would enjoy killing Money's fat ass just as much as I would. We searched high and low for Money, but he was nowhere to be found. I scoped out all the restaurants that he did business at for several days and he never showed up. I was highly disappointed that Money had pulled a disappearing act. Even though he was nowhere to be found, I still had to send him a message and what other way to do it than to kidnap his daughter?

"Yo, there she goes right there," I said, as I tapped Gunz on his shoulder while we sat outside of Money's baby mother's apartment building. I followed him to her crib a couple of times, which is why it was easy to find her. As the fine red bone got out the driver seat, switched her thickness to the back door of the car, she reached in and grabbed her daughter out the car seat. Gunz and I jumped out the minivan dressed in all black and took her child at gunpoint. I almost snapped the bitch's neck because of all the hollering and screaming she was doing. My beef wasn't with her, though, it was with her baby's daddy, so I slapped her around a couple of times before leaving her with my number to give to him.

"Listen to these instructions carefully. Tell Money that he fucked with the wrong female and if he wants to see his daughter grow up, he better call me within the next 48 hours. Let him know it's an even trade, a life for a life."

"I don't know where Money is at. I haven't seen or talked to him in a week." She sobbed in between words.

"If you know what's best for your daughter, you will find him," I stated, sternly.

With that being said, Gunz and I jumped in the rental and headed back to Chicago with Money's five-month old daughter. I decided the best way to conduct our business would be back in Chicago because, in New York, he had the upper hand. Listening to his baby cry in the back seat was giving me a damn headache. That's when I realized that I had zero tolerance for kids, especially a child of this age, so he better show up sooner than later or he will be picking out a pretty pink casket.

$$\$\$\$\$\$\$\$\$\$$

Looking at the caller ID on my phone, I saw Sparkle's number flash across. I guess she's ready for her next job. I didn't have anything lined up right now because I was too busy concentrating on seeking revenge on Money for what he did to Honeybun.

Finally picking up the phone for her, she said that she wanted to meet up because she had to talk to me about something very important. Already having an idea as to what she wanted to talk to me about, I agreed to meet up with her within the next two hours. I never got a chance to apologize to her for killing Dee-Man in front of her. I know she was freaked out when she heard my voice and I know killing him in front of her wasn't a wise idea, but he had to go. Plus, she had no business there fucking her friend's man.

Arriving at Morton's Steakhouse, we placed our orders. I ordered filet mignon, double-cut and a Porterhouse, with a glass of red wine. She ordered a New York strip steak, with a glass of white wine. At this point, I was anxious to know what she wanted to talk about, but as I said before, I had a good idea.

"What's up, shawty? What do I owe the pleasure of having this dinner with you today?"

"Ummm, ummm." It seemed like she was trying to find the right words, but couldn't.

"Ummm, ummm, what, Sparkle? Spit it out. Cat got your tongue?"

"Well, I'm sure you probably realize that I know you were the man behind that mask."

"I'm lost. What mask? What you talking about, Sparkle?" I didn't want to give in too quickly, so I decided to pick her brain to see where this conversation was going.

"J, stop playing stupid. I'm talking about Dee-Man and if you want me to keep my mouth closed, you have to pay me," she said, getting straight to the point.

I almost choked on my drink when I heard those words. "Have you lost your fucking mind? Pay you for what? So, you trying to blackmail a nigga, huh? I can't believe you, Sparkle."

"Listen, J," she spoke, taking control of the conversation. "I have to do what I have to do to survive in these streets. I'm trying to get some quick money like you. You go around robbing niggas, so I don't see why it's a problem with me robbing you, but I'm not doing it with a gun. You don't work hard to get your money and I damn sure don't want to work hard to get mines. Just like you got a hustle, I got one, so please don't knock mines. Once you pay me, you will never have to worry about seeing me again, so you got a choice here; you can either pay up or spend the rest of your life in jail."

I couldn't believe what I was hearing. I couldn't believe Sparkle was really trying to play me. Who does this bitch think she's talking to? Now I got to kill her for trying to play me like a chump. Sparkle is a snitch and I don't take too kindly to those types of people. Yeah, I got to get rid of her soon before she starts running off at the mouth about what happened when her and Buttah went to Atlanta. She has lost her mind coming at me like this. No one has ever blackmailed me and she's not going to be the first.

Still trying to pick her brain, I finally replied,

"How much money you asking for?"

A wide smile came across her face, "All I want is $150,000."

All she wants is a $150,000, I thought to myself. This bitch is crazy. She's acting like she's asking for $150. Going along with her plan, I told her that she would get the money within a week. Leading her to believe that the battle was hers, we enjoyed our food and then parted ways.

I sat in my car outside the restaurant for a couple minutes in deep thought. I couldn't believe Sparkle. I laughed to myself because I couldn't believe Sparkle had that much courage to blackmail me. Honestly, I don't want to kill the bitch, but if push comes to shove, I have no problem with putting the bitch to sleep for trying to come between me and my freedom. I think if I give her some dick, she might change her mind; then again, maybe not. I laughed to myself again. I decided to call my sis to tell her what her girl had up her sleeve.

Before Buttah said hello into the phone, she yelled, "Come and get this damn baby. I'm not a fucking babysitter." I couldn't do anything but laugh. The chick that I paid to babysit had to run a couple of errands for me, which is why Buttah was stuck with the baby.

"Okay, Buttah, ol' girl should be on her way back over there to pick up the baby and I can't believe Money hasn't called me yet to claim his seed. I guess I'll be singing rock a bye baby within the next 12 hours if I haven't heard from him by then. Enough about him, I got a problem, a major problem, and it's concerning your girl, Sparkle."

"What's going on with Sparkle?"

"She's trying to blackmail me, so she has to go."

"What you mean, blackmail you?"

"She seen me ki…you know what? I'll be over there in a bit to discuss it. I don't want to talk about it over the phone."

As soon as I hung up the phone with Buttah, a private call popped up on the caller ID of my cell phone.

"Speak."

"Nigga, how's that bitch doing?"

"You need to be less concerned about the bitch and be concerned about what's going to happen to your baby girl if you're not on the next flight to Chicago."

"I'm gonna tell you like this, if one string of hair is missing off my daughter's head, I'm gonna kill your whole fucking family. I did some research on your bitch ass. For a little bit of money, a nigga will sell his soul. I know all about the business you and your sister run and know that you two are in arm's reach. I don't have time to play with you. Just tell me how much money you want and we can get this over with."

Laughing at his ass, I stated, "Nigga, save the threats and this isn't about money. Nigga, you can keep your money; this here is much deeper than money. This is a life for a life. All you have to do is meet me to claim your prize. I'm tired of the little bitch crying anyway.

Call me when you get in town, nigga." That was the last thing I said before I hung up the phone.

Chapter Twenty-Eight
Sparkle

hat was easy, I thought to myself, as I drove away from the curb after having dinner with J. I thought I was going to have to put up a big fight with him about lowering that bread, but no man wants to sit in jail, so I knew he wouldn't have a problem with paying. I guess you can put a price on a man's freedom. Feeling a $150,000 richer, I decided to head over to Bone's house instead of going home. I was ready to spend some much needed time with him. I'm so glad he finally came to his senses. Instead of me calling him to let him know I was coming, I decided to surprise him.

Pulling up to his crib, all I could do was shake my head. There was nothing else to discuss. I confirmed what I already knew. My first reaction was to knock on his door, but I decided to stay put. As I read the license plates that read, 'His Money', I wanted badly to key Buttah's Range Rover. I knew she was fucking him. A woman's intuition is a motherfucker. Instead of pulling off, I parked three cars behind hers. Sitting and waiting patiently, I decided to call his phone to see if he would answer and, of course, he didn't. I decided to call her phone to see if she would answer and, of course, I got the same result. I couldn't take the anticipation of what might be going on in the house between the two. Going against my better judgment, I did what any scorned woman would do. I got out my car and headed to his front door. Getting half way there, I turned around. I had something better in mind, something that would definitely relieve my stress. I popped the trunk of my car and got my crowbar out. Running directly to Buttah's truck, I began to bust out her windows. One by one, the windows shattered. I didn't care who was watching; she was being disrespectful by sleeping with Bone and now it was time she felt repercussion for her actions. As soon as I started to go to work on her front windshield, she came running out the door. She charged me, knocking my back against the hood of her truck. The crowbar went flying out my hand from the unexpected rush. Our grown asses were fighting like we didn't know each other. I had to make her believe that fat meat is greasy. There was weaves flying everywhere. She wasn't as tough as she portrayed herself. I beat the shit of Buttah. Bone didn't try to stop us from fighting, either. Actually, it seemed he was enjoying every moment. After I got tired of beating her ass, I picked up the crowbar from the ground and charged at him. His reflex was a motherfucker because he grabbed the crowbar out my hand and knocked me right on my ass.

I knew I couldn't beat Bone, but I had to get my point across. "You nasty dick bastard, I hope you two motherfuckers burn in hell," I stated, as I picked up a bottle off the ground and threw it at him. Buttah wasn't finished, though. She had the perfect opportunity to attack and she did just that. While I was still on the ground, she kicked the shit out of me. She kicked and she kicked until Bone began to see the hurt in my face. He picked her up by the waist and they both went into the house as if nothing ever happened.

Chapter Twenty-Nine
BUTTAH

So much has been going on in my life that I never got a chance to get up with Doughboy. He called me on several occasions, but I was always in a situation where I couldn't talk. I really wanted to make him my man, but time is not on my side. J-Boogie has been putting his master plan in motion for the set-up of Doughboy, so I have no other choice but to ride with my brother. Besides trying to be with Doughboy, I had major problems in my life. I still have this damn baby growing inside of me. I missed my appointment, so I had to schedule another one. I still don't know how that pregnancy test came back negative that Bone had given me. Then I have this love triangle situation with Bone; he just won't let me go. All this stuff is making me stressed, but I can't let any of my current situations get the best of me because when it all boils down, there is money that still needs to be made. On top of all this, Sparkle fucked up my $70,000 truck. I was going to save her ass from J-Boogie, but he can do whatever the fuck he wants to do with her now. I can't believe she let dick come between us. If I'm not fucking him, she had better believe another chick is.

Sitting on Bone's couch, I didn't say a word to him. I had a lot on my mind, but a smile came across my face immediately following my next thought.

"Now that Sparkle knows about us that means you can't force me to fuck with you anymore, so guess what, nigga? Today will be your last time seeing this face. My time is too precious to be laid up with you," I stated, as I got off the couch to retrieve my car keys from his cocktail table. Just thinking about my truck gave me a headache. I can't believe I have to drive down the streets with broken windows; furthermore, I can't believe what Sparkle did to my car.

"Sit down and get undressed. Where do you think you going without giving me some pussy? All this stuff you talking about you not messing with me any-more needs to stop. You not fooling anybody but your-self because it's not over until I say it's over and guess what? It will never be over." Bone spoke harshly to me.

I didn't feel like fighting with Bone, so I gave him some mind blowing pussy for the last time. After I left out his front door, he would never see me again.

SSSSSSSSS

Calling J-Boogie, I filled him in on the incident

with Sparkle. He filled me in on the situation with him and her as well. It hurt like hell that he was going to kill her because she has been like a sister to me. We shared some great moments together, but J's freedom was in jeopardy, so there was no time to get sentimental. Bottom line is, Sparkle had to go.

Sitting at my kitchen table, enjoying a homemade turkey sandwich, I rubbed my stomach and thought about what it would be like to be a mother. My mother was a good mother to me, so I know I would be a wonderful mother to my child. I just hate I had to get pregnant by Bone and especially at this time in my life. I was too busy chasing the dead white men around to be committed to a child. My phone interrupted my mother and child moment. It was Honeybun. I haven't talked to her since we made it back to Chicago.

"Hey, chica, how you feeling?"

"I'm feeling okay, despite the circumstance. I just wanted to let you know that I will be moving within the next two weeks. I just need to finish some unfinished business before I make this move. There is nothing left for me in Chicago. I think it's best that I start over in another state."

"There is plenty here in Chicago, girl; I'm here," I stated, trying to lighten the mood. Her voice was shaky when she was talking to me, so I knew something major was going on in her life that she didn't care to share at this time. I never was the one to press a person into telling me something they were uncomfortable with.

"You right; you are here and that's why I will come back every chance I get."

What the hell? I might as well press her a little bit, "What's the matter, Honeybun; do you care to talk about it?"

I could tell she was crying on the other end of the phone by now. "Naw, Buttah, now is not the time; but, I promise you, I will let you know what's going on. Just let me get out of Chicago first." After that, all I heard was a dial tone in my ear.

Something deep must be really going on with Honeybun, but before I was able to think more about Honeybun's situation, my phone rings. Now what the hell could J possibly want? I just got off the phone with him.

"It's show time," J-Boogie stated. I knew he was talking about Money being in town to claim his prized possession, his daughter.

"Okay, you do know you have to come pick me up because I'm truckless for now."

"Oh, damn, I forgot. I'm on my way," he laughed, like I was telling a joke.

Jumping in the car with J, he had Gunz with him and the baby was well secured in a car seat that I know one of his chicks let him borrow. The baby was a cute little girl. She didn't have a care in the world. She had the perfect curly hair and the fattest cheeks. At this moment, I rubbed my stomach again. "Mommy loves you, but you will never get a chance to see this world," I spoke quietly to myself.

"What you back there talking about, Buttah?" J-Boogie asked.

"Nothing at all; I was playing with the baby."

Gunz all of a sudden blurted out, "I'm ready to lay this nigga to rest. My trigger finger is very itchy."

"Mines, too, my nigga," J spoke.

"What's the plan, J," I stated, curious as to how things are going to go down.

"There's no plan. I'm sure he will have his people with him, so y'all be alert. First opportunity I get, I'm shooting his ass dead. We don't have anything to talk about. I already told him a life for a life."

Pulling up behind Brach's old candy factory, there was a black Hummer with tinted windows parked, awaiting us. As J-Boogie reduced the speed of the car, we caught a park right next to it. I reached in my purse to retrieve my gun. I was uneasy about this situation because I couldn't make out how many people were in the vehicle next to ours. For a good three minutes, we sat in the car and so did Money. J decided to call Money. Once Money picked up J stated, "Let's do business." I was to stay put in the car with the baby, but was instructed to get in the driver seat in case anything went wrong. J wanted me to drive off with the baby and kill her if anything seemed out of place. I really didn't want to kill the baby, but her daddy chose this lifestyle and he knows what came along with it, meaning death and sacrifices. Being aware of my surroundings, I placed my chrome on my lap, prepared for anything to go down.

When Money got out the car, he had on a bulletproof vest and two other niggas with him. Money wasn't prepared to die; he was prepared to get his daughter back and prepared for war. Each one of his guys had guns in both of their hand and so did Money. The situation wasn't looking good for us. It wasn't in our favor at all. Why we only came three strong beats the hell out of me. Listening to the conversation outside the car, I continued to focus on my surroundings.

"Are you ready for the exchange," J stated, with much confidence. He didn't care if he was outnumbered. He was a soldier with great gun experience.

"Naw, nigga, no exchange. These are the rules, homie. You give me back my daughter and I let you live." That right there should have been my cue to leave, but I stayed put because I knew J had everything under control.

Raising his gun and aiming it at Money's head, J stated, "Nope, it's not going down like that-my game and my rules. I told you how this was going down and if you can't go by my rules, all I have to do is say the word and your baby girl is dead."

Money begins to laugh. He wasn't fazed by J's threats and soon after that, Gunz raised his gun as well, but it wasn't toward Money, it was aimed directly at J's head. Shit had just gotten real. I tried starting up the car, but I was now face to face with a black piece. I was snaked. Where did this big black motherfucker come from? All he said was to give him the baby. He didn't have to ask twice. I reached in the back seat, unbuckled the car seat, and handed him the baby. He instructed me to get out the car and snatched my gun from me. The shit that was transpiring in front of my face was unbelievable. I never saw this coming and I'm sure J never saw it, either. Gunz sold us out. He had been down with the team for years and he does this shit to us. If I make it out of this shit, I swear I'm going to hunt Gunz down my damned self and give him exactly what he deserves, which is a torturous death.

I saw nothing but pure hurt in J's eyes. He never suspected his buddy to turn on him the way that he did. All of a sudden, I felt a cramp in my stomach. I guess my baby knew me and his or hers days were numbered.

"So, you the nigga that Money was talking about, huh, Gunz? You bitch ass nigga." That was the beginning and the end of their conversation because Gunz never replied; all he did was pull the trigger and J-Boogie's body hit the concrete so hard that his head cracked open. There was no doubt about it. I was next. Gunz couldn't let me live. He knows the type of woman I am. He aimed the gun at me and darkness was all there was left to see.

Chapter Thirty
NINO

*B*eing surprised when I proposed to Boo was an understatement. She cried her eyes out when I got on bended knee. The moment I set for her was perfect. The house was super clean, candles were burning, and the music was playing softly as she walked in the house from a long day of work. She had no idea that I wanted to spend the rest of my life with her and I was ready to show her off to the world. All she ever wanted was for me to be comfortable in my own skin when I was with her. I was so used to people seeing me with Honeybun that I thought I couldn't be comfortable with anyone else.

Once Boo finally calmed down from the excitement of me proposing to her, I told her to get dressed so we could go out to celebrate and after that, we were headed to my mom's house so I could introduce them to each other for the first time. I know my mother was going to have a fit once she sees who my fiancé is. She didn't want to see me with nobody, but Honeybun. She thought Honeybun could do no wrong and since she didn't have a daughter and Honeybun didn't have a mother, they shared a special bond with each other. At this point, I had to focus on me. Even though I didn't want to see my mom with a frown on her face, I had to do what made me happy. I know I was making the right decision by keeping Boo by my side. She was wonderful in all aspects. She was the perfect mate.

Sitting in the restaurant listening to the live band perform, Boo and I were enjoying each other's company when my phone began to dance in my pocket from the vibration. I ignored it the first couple of times it vibrated because I didn't want Boo's and my moment to be disturbed. After a couple more vibrations, I decided to answer.

"What's up?" I spoke into the phone.

"Dawg, why haven't you been answering your phone? I've been calling you back to back, nonstop. That bitch you had me watching finally showed up. I think she was out of town; that's why she has been MIA. When she walked through the door, she had luggage and shit."

"Good looking, homie. Good looking. I'm on my way."

"Naw, dawg, she's gone again."

"What you mean, she's gone? You just said she was there."

"Man, I've been calling your phone for the last hour and you didn't answer. She eventually left the house. I tried trailing her but, somehow, I lost her in traffic."

"Damn, I can't believe this shit," I stated, as I hit the table. Boo grew a concerned look on her face. She didn't know what was going on. I know she was wondering what had me so upset when we were sharing a special moment together. "Go back to Honeybun's house and as soon as you see her again, call my phone and I'll be on my way."

Hearing Honeybun's name was enough confirmation for Boo. She knew what was going on so there was no need to ask questions. Boo wanted so badly to beat up Honeybun, but I wouldn't allow it and plus, it wouldn't be a fair fight. Boo would've hurt that girl and even though I wanted her hurt, I wanted to be the one to do it. It wasn't her fight; it was mine.

Not trying to let my phone conversation ruin my proposal celebration with Boo, I focused in on her and told her all the sweet things she wanted and deserved to hear. She listened closely as she fondled the three-karat ring that I diligently placed on her hand earlier that day. That ring look amazing. It was a perfect fit for my perfect queen.

"Daddy, let's get out of here," Boo spoke. "I need you in my mouth ASAP."

I knew I was marrying the right person. I definitely had a freak on my hands. We didn't even get a chance to place an order for food. I grabbed Boo's hand and we walked out the door, not caring who saw us together. Today was definitely a new beginning for me. It was the beginning of my road for everlasting happiness. There was nothing anyone could do to me today that would steal my joy. My day would be even more complete if I got my hands on Honeybun. Her time is approaching and when it does, she going to reap what she sowed.

Driving through traffic, Boo was giving me some of the best head that any mouth could offer. Her head game was magnificent. I almost crashed the car a couple of time as she performed like a professional in the field of fellatio. Once I came to a complete stop at a red light, it seems like she really put her neck into it. There were no complaints coming from my end. Not being able to keep my composure, I rotated my hips as I fucked her in her mouth. I closed my eyes for a brief moment, while my toes curled up on the brake pedal and my driver hand held tightly around the steering wheel. I felt the tingling sensation building up inside of me and I was ready to bust in Boo's mouth at any given moment. She continued to work her mouth up and down, while trying to get me to the point of no return then, all of a sudden, my dick went limp. I couldn't believe it. I begin to feel nervous and anxious at the same time. Nervous because I didn't want Honeybun to see me in the position I was in and anxious because I had her at my fingertip. Still glancing over in her car, she still hadn't noticed she had pulled up on the side of me. She was too busy looking straight ahead as she watched some girl carry a baby on her hip crossing the street while she pushed another baby in the stroller. Honeybun looked stressed for some reason and her facial expression showed she had a lot on her mind. I could definitely tell she lost a couple of pounds just by staring in her face. Trying to keep Boo's head down and not wanted her to come up, I put my hand on top of her head. Why did I do that? Boo hated for me to touch her head while she was giving me head. When she rose up, she made eye contact with Honeybun and right after that, all hell broke loose.

Honeybun threw her car in park and jumped out, not caring how many cars were behind her in traffic. She yelled to the top of her lungs, "What the fuck is going on? You faggot ass niggas."

Not caring that the light had changed to green, I threw my car in park also. I got out and Boo wasn't too far behind me because we both despised the faggot word. Cars were honking their horns at us as we made a scene on North Ave in the middle of the street. I was ready to kill the bitch. I didn't care how many witnesses were around. It was time that I give Honeybun was she deserved. Honeybun had violated me on so many levels. Faggot or not, I was still a man and she had to respect me as such.

Honeybun was yelling all types of foolish stuff, but what caught my attention was when she kept referring to Boo as Kane. I was looking like 'who the fuck is Kane?', but I'll cross that bridge in a minute. Since Honeybun was in arms reach, I stretched my arm out and started choking her. I was tired of hearing her voice and it was time I cut off her oxygen for good. Honeybun wasn't going down without a fight, though. Lately, she had come across this super woman strength. She started swinging at me. Her punches weren't fazing me until she hit me in my damn eye. I broke the grip from around her neck and held onto my eye.

Catching her breath, she started to speak again. "Kane, your old ass nasty as hell. We just sleep together two weeks ago and now you sucking my ex's dick. Why would you come into my life if you knew you were a dick in the booty ass nigga?" Right after that, Honeybun bent over and threw up. I'm confused like a motherfucker, but from what I've just heard, I was ready to kill them both.

"Boo, what the fuck is she talking about? Who the fuck is Kane? Explain yourself, nigga."

"Baby."

"Don't baby me," I cut Boo off. "Nigga, address me as Nino at all times."

"Just hear me out, baby, please. I went out to have breakfast at IHOP that morning after me and you had that big argument. I ran into here there. I knew you had just left me to go home to be with her and I was wondering why she was out instead of home with you. I knew you were confused about our relationship and I felt that Honeybun was the reason why you couldn't commit to me. Therefore, I took matters into my own hands. I knew if she had another person in her life that she would stop focusing so much on you and fall out of love and that would make it much easier for you to walk away from her. Believe me, baby; I did all of this for us. You know I hate pussy. I haven't slept with a woman in over 18 years." Boo whined to me like a little girl. What masculine ways he had left had just went out the window.

Getting herself together, Honeybun spoke. "Wait a minute. Wait one motherfucking minute. So, you two are together? This shit is crazy," she stated as she pinched herself to make sure she wasn't dreaming. "My eyes have to be deceiving me. This can't be real. Nino, what the hell was you thinking? You had me fooled; hell, you had everybody fooled. You two motherfuckers are sick, a disgrace to society. Nino, I can take you cheating on me with a woman, but a man, that's a low blow. You know what, nigga, I definitely have no regrets with robbing your sorry ass, you got everything you had coming to you, but check this out. Since a bomb has been dropped on me, let me drop a bomb on you two queers. You two need to go to the doctor as soon as possible. I'm HIV positive. I'm sure Kane gave it to you and Nino, you passed the disease on to me."

"HIV! Bitch, you better stop playing with me. I

have no symptoms of being sick. Look at me; I'm still 225 pounds, I haven't lost any weight. I know what your ass trying to do. Just because I'm gay, you're trying to start a rumor about me giving you that shit. You ain't nothing but a typical bitch. "

"Nino, you sound stupid as fuck. You're so un-educated about this disease it doesn't make any sense, but you don't have to believe me. What benefit will I get from saying you have HIV? There is nothing else to talk about. I said what I had to say. Just go to the doctor and get those meds if you plan on living a long life with this disease. As a matter of fact, just ask your li'l boyfriend about this. I'm sure he knows what he passed along."

Without thinking twice, I lunged toward Boo and started to beat the brakes off his ass. What love I did have for him was gone. My body was numb from head to toe from all the pain. Yes, my feminine side was kicking in. Honeybun took me for just about everything I own, my fiancé is sleeping with my ex-girlfriend, and now I'm living with HIV. What a life? As me and Boo tussled to the ground, I landed on top of him. Grabbing his head in my hands, I banged it on the concrete re-peatedly, until blood started seeping from his head. Lis-tening to the police sirens becoming closer and closer, I remained focused on Boo. I was determined to have him dead before they got there. As the onlookers looked in awe, it just made my adrenaline pump even more.

At this point, I considered my life to be over. My time on this earth was limited. I'd rather rot in jail than rot on the outside because my image is now demolished. Where did my life go wrong? I guess if I weren't living a double life, things wouldn't have turned out this way. When I met Boo two years ago, I knew that things in my life would change, but I thought it would be for the better. Look at me now. I'm about to catch a 187 and probably be in jail for the rest of my life.

Chapter Thirty-One
Honeybun

There was so much resentment built up inside of me. I wanted so badly to join in as I continued to watch Nino bang Kane's head against the concrete. With every full force contact his head made with the ground, I could see the devil riding Nino's back with a smile on his face. It looked like someone had gone on a murdering spree with all the blood covering the ground. He split his head to the white meat. The sun didn't make it any better as it cooked the blood, giving it an eerie smell. I was overjoyed when I saw Kane take his last breath, but there was still a problem. Nino was still breathing. I didn't have enough energy in me to fight at the moment, so I waited patiently for the police to do their job.

When the police finally approached the crime scene, Nino was leaning against his car smoking a blunt. He knew he was going to jail for the rest of his life. Not only was he going to jail for killing Kane, he was going to jail for transmitting that deadly disease to me. Even though Kane had taken destiny into his own hands and put two lives in jeopardy, I'm sure he wasn't expecting this to be the end of his life story. Now I'm left here distraught, thinking about what path I'm going to take with my own life. I've been through a lot with Nino these last couple of years and not once did I ever see this coming. Right when I thought I found happiness, another roadblock comes along.

If someone would have walked up to me and told me the man I once wanted to spend the rest of my life with and the man I was falling in love with were lovers, there's no way I would have believed it in a million years. Witnessing this with my own two eyes was still hard for me to fathom. I just can't believe I was sleeping with Nino all these years and didn't see any signs to him being gay. Wait a minute, now that I think about it, there were several clues. The way he would hold his hand from time to time, his oversensitive ways, his homophobic behavior, and the tell-tale signs of them all were when he lost interest in me when it came to sex. All the signs were there, but I was just too blind to see them.

$$$$$$$$$$

Dear Buttah,

If you're reading this letter, that means I'm in a more peaceful place by now. As I sit here and write my thoughts out to you, my heart is aching. I've been in a lot of pain these last couple of years and I owe all of that to Nino. Before you continue reading, if you're standing, please take a seat. Not only do I consider you as a friend, you're my family, my sister, so it's only right that I fill you in on everything so your heart won't be so heavy. When I was in the hospital, I learned that I have HIV. When the doctor smacked me in the ear with those words, I sunk into a deep state of depression. I haven't been right ever since I heard those words. To make matters even worse, the man that I was falling in love with is gay. I thought he would be the one that swept me off my feet. What's really going to have you tripping out is guess who his lover is...Nino. I know your mouth is wide open, but you are reading these words correctly, yes, Nino is Kane's lover. I caught them in traffic in the act. My heart can't take any more hurt. I've been hurt so many times, so I decided to put an end to all of this. Buttah, I'm sorry, but it's time that I go see my mother. I love you, girl, and take care.

Grabbing the stamped envelope off the counter top, I stuffed the letter inside of it and sealed it with a kiss. I knew what I was about to do was wrong, but I couldn't take living this life anymore. I turned my bottle of Remy upside down, drinking it down to the very last drop, while reflecting back on my relationship with Nino. In the beginning of our relationship, I was in it for the love of money, but soon after, I fell in love with him. When he cheated on me, I stayed just for the love of the money, and when I was fed up with him, I robbed him for every cent he had all because of my love for them Ben Franks. Now that I look at it, my love for the mighty dollar is what has me in the predicament that I'm in now. If I could turn back the hands of time, I would, because now, I know money isn't everything. Money is the root to all evil and I had to learn the hard way.

Starting up the engine of my car, I cut my eyes over at my Michael Kors bag that was full of money with a disgusted look on my face. Pulling out into traffic not paying attention, I collided with a vehicle and kept it moving. I had an appointment with my maker and I wasn't going to be late for anyone. As I drove up the street, I stopped at the mailbox and dropped Buttah's letter in it. Soon after, I was back in the car driving to my destination. I drove like I was the only one on the road, from hitting parked cars, to running lights. Before I knew it, I had hit a pedestrian and guess what? I kept it moving. I jumped on the expressway to get to down-town Chicago much quicker. I couldn't take it anymore. My heart became heavier and heavier by the minute. It was too heavy for me to carry. I was ready to end my life at that moment. I was really considering running into a brick wall as my speedometer reached 90 mph, but I voted against it quickly. I was going to stick to my original plan.

Easing off the expressway at Lake Street, I ran into some congested traffic. By this being summer time, downtown was always crowded, no matter the time of day. You had your vacationers walking around sightseeing, the residents of the city on an outing with their family, and some people leaving work. Staring at the people, it didn't look like they had a worry in the world. If they did, they were too busy enjoying themselves to let it bother them at that moment, but I, on the other hand, was a totally different story.

Finally making it to Wells Street Bridge, I leapt out my car and felt a sense of peace in my heart. The feeling was like no other and at that moment, I didn't have a care in the world. The light wind blew briskly through my hair as I had a quick flashback. I saw my mother looking beautiful in her all-white with a big smile on her face as she showed off her pearly white teeth. Then all of a sudden, my heart was saddened. This was the same bridge I watched my mother's boyfriend throw her off. Tears streamed down my face. It was finally time I do what I came there to do. My heart couldn't take another minute of hurt. I took a stand on the railing of the bridge that overlooked Lake Michigan. With my Michael Kors purse in hand, I let the money fly freely with the wind. That money is what caused me my problems so now it's can be somebody else's problem. People began to crowd around me screaming don't jump, but when they saw the money flying, they became less focused on me and intrigued with the money. Taking my last deep breath, I looked to the sky and leapt off the bridge.

Chapter Thirty-Two
Buttah

*W*rapping my arms around myself, I gave myself a big hug because I was still alive. A higher power was definitely with me. I managed to escape death. When Gunz's pistol when off, I automatically fainted as his bullet skinned the side of my head. I guess once I hit the ground, he figured I was dead and him and his partners got in the car and drove off. I'm still in total shock, though. I can't believe Gunz turned on us like that-all for the love of money. Now that J-Boogie is dead, what am I going to do? My brother was my keeper and protector. We both knew what came with the business, but thought we would be out before any one of us got hurt. I guess if you live for the love of money, you will die for the love of money. Right now, all I can do is remain focused; J wouldn't want it any other way. I've been cooped up in the house for the last couple of days thinking long and hard to see if I should go ahead with the plan of robbing Dough-Boy so I could be out this game for good. Of course, my greed for the money made my decision very easy. I also thought about my other two situations, Bone and Sparkle. Nothing has changed with Bone. He constantly blows up my phone on the daily and for Sparkle, I got her. There isn't anything like sweet revenge. I totally understand her being upset, but we are girls. Dick is never supposed to come between us. Men do this shit all the time and still can maintain a cordial relationship with their buddy if they had sex with one of their girls. I also have to get her for trying to blackmail J-Boogie.

There was a light knock on my door. Since I didn't get a ring from the front desk announcing I had a visitor, it only had to be one of two people-one of my neighbors or Sasha, which was one of the building workers that I pay to bring my mail. Checking my mailbox is the least of my concerns, so she checks it once a week for me. Opening up the door, it was Sasha. I greeted her with a smile and retrieved my mail as she stood in the doorway and chatted with me for a couple of minutes. Skimming through my mail, I noticed I had a letter from Honeybun. My mind was a little puzzled. Why would she mail me anything? Why didn't she just call me or even let me know she was mailing me something? I told Sasha I had to go and I begin to open the letter that Honeybun sent me. Before I had a chance to read the letter, I got distracted by my phone and put the letter down. Looking at the caller ID, my day was blown, it was Bone's bothersome ass. Forgetting all about the letter, I gathered my things to make a quick run, but before hitting the door, my TV caught my attention. I wasn't prepared to hear what the news anchor was about to say. Holding my hand over my mouth, I couldn't believe what I was seeing. My eyes focused in on my television and my ears tuned in as Kim Le from Fox News reported...

Three days ago tragedy struck downtown Chicago as many witnessed a young woman jump from the Wells Street Bridge. When the incident first happened, the identity of the young woman was withheld, but now it is confirmed that she was 22-year old Heidi Baker. If this story is new to you, Coast Guards resumed Heidi's body from Lake Michigan...

I didn't hear anything else after that. My brain froze instantly. I couldn't take another death; first J-Boogie, now Honeybun. Knots began to form in the pit of my stomach and I began to hyperventilate. I quickly laid down on my couch and took a couple of deep breaths so I wouldn't pass out. My mind went back to three days ago. I rode past that bridge as I was going home. I saw the crowd of people, but kept it moving because whatever was happening wasn't any of my business; shame on me. Maybe if I would have gotten out the car to be nosey, I could have saved my friend. Building up enough courage, I grabbed the letter off the table. As my eyes ran across each word, tears leaked from my eyes. I totally sympathize with her situations, but what I don't agree with is her taking her life. Now I'm stuck here grieving over two people that were dear to my heart. I lost them both in a matter of days. I simply closed my eyes and went into a deep sleep so I could have sweet dreams about J-Boogie and Honeybun.

$$$$$$$$

"Sparkle, I know I fucked up. I really do apologize, but we need to squash this shit. We are all we got. J-Boogie is gone and so is Honeybun. I can't take all three of you being out my life. I'm coming to you as a woman. I'm sorry and I mean that from the bottom of my heart," I spoke into the phone.

"Listen, Buttah, you fucked me over too many times. I'm not sure if I'll be able to forgive you for this. You made your bed, so now you have to lie in it. You are one conniving bitch and I don't think I could ever be your friend again. You betrayed me too many times and it was all over some dick. Friends don't do each other like that. With a friend like you, why do I need enemies?" She stated with a stern voice.

"I totally understand, but I'm hurting right now. I need you. I'm begging you. I'm sorry. I fucked up and I know it. Please don't let Bone come between us. I promise you, I will never do anything else to hurt…"

Cutting me off as if I was nobody, she spoke, "See, it's bitches like you who make it hard for bitches

like me to trust anybody. I forgave you one too many
times and look what you go and do. You do it all over
again. Do you have any self-respect? Buttah, I really do
hate your guts. Fuck that, I hate your soul. You're a nobody to me right now. We will never ever be friends
again. Bye, Buttah"

"Wait, Sparkle; please don't hang up the phone.
Since you don't want to be my friend, I do have a prop-
osition for you. Then, after this, you don't have to say
anything else to me. I need your help. We can make a
lot of money on this last robbery and after this, we can
walk away from each other for good. Believe me when I
tell you, it's a lot of fucking money to be made. I know
you need the money because J-Boogie told me all about
you trying to blackmail him."

"I'm listening."

"Just meet me at my crib in an hour and I'll go
over everything with you."

"Okay and please don't think once that me and
you are back friends; I'm in this for the love of money
and that's it," Sparkle shouted.

I can't believe Sparkle was trying to be stub-
born. Begging any bitch is out of my character and she
knows that, but I had to do what I had to do so things
can go according to plan.

When Sparkle arrived at the house, I went over
the plan. Dough-boy was our target and once we got at
him and I killed her, I was moving far away from Chicago. Yes, I said kill her. What I hated most is a snitch

ass bitch and plus, she fucked up my car. I haven't forgot about that. Yeah, it's petty, but messing with me and
the ones I love will bring the devil out of me. There was
nothing left in Chicago for me, just far too many
memories that I can't bear and plus, this will give me
the opportunity to get away from Bone and finally get
rid of this baby.

Sparkle spoke up and stated that she knew another way that we could start the healing process between us. I laughed to myself because she was just saying how much she hated me, but I listened attentively as
she told me how she wanted to have one last threesome
with me. I knew this girl was infatuated with me, but
damn. She mentioned that the guy was willing to give
us a $1,000 apiece. She had sex with him a couple of
times and she said the D is good. Once she said the D
was good, I was in. I hate for a good dick to go to waste
and after I get rid of her, maybe when I come back to
Chicago for visits, he will be my fuck buddy.

$$\$\$\$\$\$\$\$\$\$$

Walking into the Ritz Carlton Hotel, I was ready
to get this over with. I was looking forward to the next
day, so I could go on with my plans on robbing Dough-
Boy. Like I said before, Dough-Boy has reached out to
me on several occasions, but I was just too busy to entertain him at the time. I knew that this day would
come, so I made sure I gave him enough phone conversation to hold his attention.

Catching the elevator to the 15th floor, I looked over at Sparkle and saw she was in awe. Sometimes, I think this girl hasn't been off the block. She is so amused at certain things. Yes, this was a nice hotel, but a female of my status has been to nicer places. I lived not too far from the hotel, so the same view this hotel has, I have from my apartment.

Knocking on the door, we were greeted by a tall, fine, chocolate man with dreads. I must say chocolate and dreads are my weakness. He was taller than the normal and nicely built. He walked right passed us heading out the door. We made eye contact for a brief second and he yelled, "I'll get back with you later, boss man, and by the way, have fun with these fines ass bitches."

Walking into the hotel room, I was in shock to see who the boss man was. It was Dough-Boy. For a brief moment, I thought she was trying to set me up, but I never disclosed the name of the person we were setting up. I know exactly where this was going. Sparkle knew that I had an interest in him. I guess this is her way of getting me back for fucking her guys. Being here with Dough-boy could actually turn out to be a good thing, though. The wheels in my head got to turning and I was ready to get this show on the road. He smiled when he saw me. Then I saw the reaction on Sparkle's face and it wasn't a good one. She wasn't expecting him to warm up to me like that. I know she wanted to betray me as a hoe, but the difference between me and any other hoe is, I'm a classy hoe.

Getting right down to what we were there for, I assumed the position and so did Sparkle. In the middle of our big orgy, the door was kicked in and in came a man with a mask on his face with his gun in hand. The first thing that popped in my head was the masked man was there to rob Dough-Boy, but when he told him to put on his clothes and leave quickly and quietly, my heart dropped to the bottom of my stomach. All I could think about was all the people I've robbed and the tables had finally turned. When I looked over at Sparkle, she didn't show any type of reaction and that wasn't like her. If my memory serves me correctly, dude came straight toward me and knocked me out with the butt of his gun and the next thing I knew, I'm tied up to a bed post being held hostage by this deranged bastard.

I didn't know it was Bone who was holding me hostage until I was conscious. I tried screaming, but my mouth was taped shut. He noticed me trying to yell, but the only thing he did was laugh while taking off his mask. When I saw his face, I knew that it was the end of the road for me. He was obsessed with me and he didn't want to see me with anybody else but him. If he couldn't have me, then no one else would.

I glanced around the room to see if the place looked familiar and it didn't. Fear took over my mind as I began to panic. Still glancing around the room, I noticed that it looked old and reeked of piss. It seemed as if I was in an abandoned attic because when I held my head up, I noticed a window and all I could see was the sky and the top of some trees. I cursed myself repeatedly for ever sleeping with his psychotic ass.

Several minutes had passed before he untaped my mouth. He sat on the bed rubbing his hand alongside my face. Shaking uncontrollably from the fear, I closed my eyes, wishing I were someplace besides there. Tears began to form in my eyes and trickled down my face. He leaned in toward me, causing me to jump a little and licked each one of my tears away. He was getting a kick out of being in control.

"Bone, please let me go, pleaseeeee," I pleaded and begged over and over until he grabbed me by my neck, cutting my words and breath short. Right before I went unconscious, he let my neck go and I began coughing. More tears began to well up in the corner of my eyes, not from the fear of dying, but from the thought of me dying by his hands. I can't believe this is happening to me.

"There's no getting out of this, Buttah. You drove me to this. I love you and this is how you repay me by sleeping with my brother." *Brother,* I thought to myself. I never slept with his brother; furthermore, I didn't even know he had a brother. Could Dough-Boy be his brother? Maybe that's why he just allowed him to put on his clothes to leave. He really had my mind puzzled, but at this point, I didn't even care. All I cared about was being free.

"Bone, please let me go," I pleaded again.

"Hell naw, bitch, you gon' die tonight. You've played with my heart and mind one too many times. I tried to show you how much I love and want to be with you and you couldn't see it 'cause you were too busy being a hoe. I tried giving you the lifestyle that every girl dreams of, but you refused to accept it. Now you leave me no other choice. You don't deserve to live."

When he made that last statement, I began to pray. *Our father which art in heaven, hallowed be thy name, thy kingdom come, thy will be done, on earth as it is in heaven...* When Bone heard me praying, he raised his hand and punched me in my mouth. My lips swelled instantly.

"Can't no prayer save you! Bitch, I'm your GOD. You were put on this earth to be with me and only me. There are only two ways out of this, Buttah. Either you live happily ever after with me, or you die and go to hell and I'll see you when I get there. Take your pick."

I know I did a lot of devious stuff throughout my life, but I didn't deserve the shit that Bone was putting me through. I looked him dead in his eyes and spit in his face. Laughing uncontrollably, Bone wiped the spit from his face and hit me with his pistol. Once again, I was out for the count.

Being unconscious for what seem like days I woke up to Sparkle having a conversation with Bone while I was still tied up to the bed post. What the fuck is going on I thought to myself. I didn't let them know that I was awake. I just laid there listening closely as they conversed with one another.

"Bone, this isn't the way we planned for this shit to go down. You weren't supposed to fall in love with the hoe. Like I told you before, Buttah is one of the reasons why my brother got killed. Her and her bitch ass brother robbed him blind then left him for dead a couple of years ago. I've been trying to get close to her for the last couple of years, but when your brother invited her into the bed with us, that was the perfect opportunity to befriend her and it worked. It took me a minute to get close to her, but she let me in eventually. She left a permanent scar on my heart. All you had to do is get close to her so we could get the money and kill her like she did my brother, but naw, you fucked, and then fell in love. Even after Marcus showed you the tape, your stupid ass went back to her."

"Listen, Sparkle, fuck what you talking about. It is what it is. If you wasn't busy being a hoe, I never would have fallen for another woman and stuck to the damn plan. The first couple of weeks we were dating you told me the lowdown on her. I was all game until you messed up. Catching you with that nigga dick in your mouth is what made me look at you differently. Furthermore, I didn't need the bread that you were offering me. There is a lot that you still don't know about me. I keep telling you that, but I wasn't about to turn down no type of money no matter how much money I have. You wanted to pay me off thinking I was going to look past the hurt in my heart that you caused me. Then right when I wanted to consider looking past what you did, Marcus showed me the tape of you having a threesome with him. Girl, you better be glad I didn't kill your ass for that shit. I don't have anything to do with you and Buttah situation no more. You messed that all up so since you're after her for your own selfish reasons, you should have been took care of her."

"Yeah, you right, I am after Buttah for my own reason, but I wouldn't call it selfish. Nigga, do you know the definition of a plan? I'm sure you do, but what I'm really tripping off of is you can't look past me having a threesome with your brother, but you can look past Buttah having a threesome with him. I understand that you weren't fucking her when he showed you the first tape, but when he showed you the second tape, y'all was deep into y'all so called relationship."

Still listening attentively, I was beyond shocked. My blood was boiling at this point. I couldn't believe these two sick motherfuckers. All along, they were plotting against me. Sparkle knew all about me and she played me like she hadn't the slightest clue as to who I was and what I was doing. She definitely had me fooled and who was her brother? Hell, we have killed so many people that I can't begin to pinpoint which one she was related to.

"Sparkle, I'm not trying to hear this shit you're talking. Just leave. I don't need you here with me. Our deal was off a long time ago. The business I have with Buttah is personal."

"Bone, Sparkle, what the fuck is going on?" I shouted to let them know I was alert and heard everything they said. Both of their heads turned in my direction at the sound of my voice. Never getting the response I was looking for, all I heard was, "Ahhhh, you crazy bitch." Sparkle took a knife and plunged it into Bone's back causing him to hit the floor. Sparkle stabbed him repeatedly until he took his last breath.

Chapter Thirty-Three
Sparkle

illing Bone was something that I didn't want to do, but it had to be done. As my knife penetrated his skin, it felt good knowing that if I couldn't have him, no one else would. He knew how much I loved him and wanted him in my life. All he had to do was allow me to make up for the wrong that I've done and we could have lived happily ever after.

After watching Bone take his last breath, it was time to take care of Buttah. She didn't deserve to live. She took away the only person who truly loved me which was my brother Shawn. About five years ago, my brother came across her at a teeny bobber club that I used to hang at. He was there to pick me up because he hated me to walk the streets. He was intrigued by the young beauty when he first laid his eyes on her. Buttah knew my brother wanted her by the way he undressed her with his eyes. I sat back in the cut and observed them while they exchanged numbers.

Buttah wasn't from my neighborhood, so I asked a couple of my buddies if they knew her. When my buddy Danielle replied yeah, she gave me the low down on her and I told my brother on my way home what I'd heard. I'm not sure if he didn't care or he didn't believe me, all I know is a couple days later, I saw her and J-Boogie leaving his house. After they drove off, I ran on the porch only to find his door wide open and him lying lifeless in the middle of the living room floor. From the stories Danielle told me, I knew Buttah was the bait. I cried over my brother's body, promising him that I would get his revenge no matter how long it took.

Now I stand here face to face with the enemy. I'm ready to give her the punishment that she deserves. My heart has been aching all these years and now it's time for the pain to stop. I untied her from the bed post and smacked the daylights out of her. I wanted her to fight for her life instead of me just taking it. Her facial expressions showed a mixture of fear and anger. I never saw her show fear. I was relishing the moment, so I smacked her again. Soon after, she got to swinging. That's all I was waiting on. Going toe to toe with her, I was determined not to let her get the best of me and I was doing a good job of it. Buttah wasn't so tough without her gun and I knew it. We fought and fought until she tripped me and I fell on the floor. Before she had a chance to get on top of me, I lifted my right leg kicking her in the stomach with all my strength. She flew back into the wall and instantly blood gushed from between her legs turning her all white linen pant into crimson red. Bending over while holding her stomach, she screamed in pain, "My baby, my baby." Not caring about her unborn child and becoming more pissed at the thought that she might be carrying Bone's child, it was time that I send her and her bastard child to hell.

Buttah was down and out at this point, still screaming from the pain that her body was encountering. Her life has always been a game. How can she sleep at night playing with people lives like it's a board game and if things didn't go according to plan, death was soon to follow? Not having a conscience is why she doesn't deserve to live any longer. I walked over to my purse to retrieve my gun. Bad as I needed all that money Buttah had come into over the course of the years, what made me happier is seeking revenge on behalf of my brother. Getting the money wasn't even a priority anymore. She lived for the love of money, not me. There was nothing else left for me to do at this point. I cried tears of joy as I loaded my brother's gun one bullet at a time while repeating the words, "Big brah, I told you I had your back." I was so ready to put this all behind me and to live a normal life.

Before loading the last bullet in the chamber, the gun hit the floor, causing all the bullets to fall out and each one rolling in a different direction. A sharp pain invaded my body. I raised my hand to touch the back of my neck. Warmness flowed down my shirt. When I finally turned around, I couldn't believe it. Bone was standing in front of me with the same knife I stabbed him with. How could this be? I stabbed him several time in the back. I saw him take his last breath, or so I thought. He was bloody as hell resembling the girl Carrie on her prom night. I knew his time was short. If an ambulance wasn't there rescuing him within the next five minutes, he was sure to be dead. He began to spit up blood while trying to say something to me and at that point, I began to feel dizzy. Not able to get his words fully out, Bone hit the floor. This time taking his last breath for sure.

As I looked around the spinning room, I saw my reflection in the window. I was bleeding badly myself from the one stab wound. Buttah was still in the corner bleeding just as badly from between her legs. I was still out to complete my mission. Walking toward her, I begin to feel weaker and weaker the closer I got to her, so I dropped to my knees and crawled in her direction while picking up my brother's gun and loading one bullet in the chamber. I had to keep my promise to my brother. I couldn't die before her. That was not possible. Pointing my gun in her direction, I aimed and then shot. I didn't hear her moaning in agonizing pain anymore. I knew I completed my mission. There was not an ounce of energy left in me, so I laid flat on my back, let the gun hit the floor, and put my hands together so I could pray and ask God for forgiveness. I asked him to forgive

me for all the wrong that I done, but I had to have justice. Street justice.

62661596R00165

Made in the USA
Lexington, KY
13 April 2017